RICHARD SHERIDAN

The author was born in Chelsea in 1962. He was expelled from school in 1977. He has been a drummer, song-writer and record producer. He is married and lives in London. His second novel is called ECHOES OF ESTHER.

Richard Sheridan

END OF '77

Copyright © Richard Sheridan, 1986

First published in Great Britain in 1986 by Chatto & Windus Ltd.

Sceptre edition 1988

Sceptre is an imprint of Hodder and Stoughton Paperbacks, a division of Hodder and Stoughton Ltd.

British Library C.I.P.

Sheridan, Richard, *1962 –*
    End of '77.
    I. Title
    823′.914[F]

    ISBN 0-340-42857-0

Printed and bound in Great Britain for Hodder and Stoughton Paperbacks, a division of Hodder and Stoughton Ltd., Mill Road, Dunton Green, Sevenoaks, Kent TN13 2YA (Editorial Office: 47 Bedford Square, London WC1B 3DP) by Richard Clay Ltd., Bungay, Suffolk.

To Paddy, Dulan and Barb

One

We don't need you, we don't need you, we don't need you, any of you.

Chrissy picked her teeth with a dead match absent-mindedly.

She was either playing it cool, not wanting him to get a swell head, or she didn't like the record and was trying to spare his feelings. What a bloody predicament. Jack's entire musical career depended on the critical opinions of his maiden bloody aunt. At thirty-five she had one foot in the grave by any self-respecting punk's standard and yet her radio show was the most popular daytime music programme in London, controlling and manipulating the taste of millions of record buyers. What she knew about punk rock you could write on the tip of a gnat's cock and still have room enough for the complete works of William Shakespeare.

'Is that it?'

Typical, absolutely sodding typical. Without even commenting on the musical or political content of the record she was already finding fault.

'Okay, so the average single lasts for three and a half minutes and ours runs for just under two. So what?'

'So, the programme directors plan for the amount of records that are played, based on an average length. If a record differs radically from –'

'"Bohemian Rhapsody" was seven minutes long and went to number one,' Jack declared triumphantly, wishing he'd found a slightly hipper example.

Chrissy sighed. 'Queen were an established band by then. People were ready to accept it.'

'Oh I see, I see, and until you're established you have to toe the line, kiss arse and grin like an idiot, is that it?'

'Yeah, okay. If that's the way you want to put it.'

If there was one thing Jack hated even more than lame excuses it was a gutless, spineless refusal to continue the argument. An argument that he was unquestionably winning. 'You just don't like it, do you? Admit it, that's the real reason why a record doesn't get on the play-list – because you just don't like it.'

'That's about the size of it.'

God how infuriating, to sit there calmly and confess to such a selfish ego trip. An anonymous-looking album lay on the floor beneath the turn-table and Jack slipped out the record and put it on.

'Mm this is nice, what is it?' Chrissy began clicking her fingers to the walking double bass and the shooshing, flicking sound of brushes sweeping back and forth across a tight snare drum.

'One of Otto's.'

Considering his position as guitarist and co-founder of The Destroyers, Jack's flatmate had an unhealthy obsession with beatnik life circa 1958 and insisted on buying music from that era. When they first formed the group Otto had even referred to their music as jazz-punk, to Jack's utter revulsion, and still gave Django Reinhardt credit for being his major influence. Otto was four years older than Jack and, at twenty, thought by his parents to be responsible. After deciding to move permanently to Amsterdam, they handed him the lease of their rented St James's apartment and wished him well. The seventy-five pounds a week rent needed to be divided three ways in order to make it possible for Otto to carry on living there, so Jack jumped at the chance to move in. Grace arrived shortly afterwards.

'How are the two love birds?' Chrissy asked as she pored over the album's sleeve notes.

'They're not sleeping together anymore. Grace has moved into the spare room.'

The original deal was that while they looked for a third person to share, Otto and Jack split the rent down the middle. Then one day Grace showed up and, unlike the other female traffic, stayed put. Though she used electricity and gas and all the rest of it, as long as she slept in Otto's room she didn't qualify as a proper tenant. Until now.

'You don't really get on with her, do you?'

That was the understatement of the millennium. He and Otto had a buddy-buddy sort of friendship and it depended on doing things together. Playing in the group and birding it down the Roebuck was what life was all about. On a good night, and there were plenty, Jack would feel the wind whip through his hair as Otto manoeuvred the crumpet wagon swiftly down the King's Road and he would know that, at that moment, nobody in the entire world was happier than he. Grace was a minor spanner in the works but nothing to get het up about.

'Sometimes I find it's hard to keep my mouth shut –'

'You can say that again,' Chrissy joked.

'No, I mean when I see how she puts the squeeze on Otto, I dunno, it seems to hurt me more than it does him. Shit, who cares? Let's talk about something else, huh? When are you finally gonna settle down, start breeding?'

Chrissy smiled and stared off into space, lost in her own private world. Jack had seen her like this one or two times recently and he didn't know what it meant. 'Just kidding,' he apologised. 'Actually, I couldn't care less, I mean who –'

'That's all right Jack.' She was gradually floating back down to earth. 'I understand.'

The jazz LP came to an end and, as Jack got up to turn it over, the phone rang.

'Helloo. Helloooo.' An absurdly exaggerated Irish accent wailed tremulously in Jack's ear. It sounded like a man's falsetto doing an awful impersonation of a woman's voice. Now who would try to pull a stunt like that? 'Hellooo, hellooo,' the wailing continued. Not Otto, it wasn't his style, this sort of gag was way too broad for him. Crude slapstick could – wait a minute – that magic word, crude.

'Andy?' asked Jack tentatively.

A roar of laughter burst from the receiver. 'Fuckinell man, how d'you guess?'

3

Andy Mason had been one of the brightest kids in Jack's class at school but he was also a villain. If anything went missing, send for Andy Mason. Gym kits, teacher's wallets, typewriters, calculators and musical instruments all mysteriously disappeared during lessons given to form 13 or, as in the case of the vanishing soldering iron, the boys of form 13. His expulsion was dramatic. A student teacher was sent to hospital to have seven stitches in his head as a result of Andy's misguided attempt to defend himself from a clip round the ear.

'I came out last Tuesday. I've just been sortin' a few fings and now they're sorted, I thought I'd come and see me old mate.'

'Come out? From where?'

'Borstal, where d'you fink?'

It had all seemed okay when they were kids but now Andy frightened Jack. 'How did you get this number?' he said, trying to sound as though he didn't give a damn.

'I got your old dear, Natalie is it? Yeah, she told me where you were, jammy sod. Saint fucking James's ay? Well I never.'

Momentarily, Jack was at a loss for words.

'Aren't you gonna invite me over then?' Andy cackled mischievously.

Better to get it over with straight away, thought Jack. It was either that or leave the country.

'Who was that?' Concern was written in capital letters all over Chrissy's forehead. 'It was that Mason boy wasn't it? What's he done now? Killed somebody I shouldn't wonder.' Her voice had acquired a frosty edge and a hint of her native, northern twang. 'He's no good for you that boy, no good at all.'

Closing his eyes Jack breathed deeply. Ten thirty in the morning was much too early for a heavy lecture on how to choose one's friends.

Chrissy changed the subject. 'How's Natalie?'

One thing Jack really liked about his aunt, she always knew when to let up.

'Fine, as far as I know. Haven't really seen her lately.' Natalie wasn't like other people's mums. She had an amazing talent for not breathing down her son's neck, leaving him free to get on

4

with his own life but, if he ever needed help, she was there in a flash. And Chrissy was the same.

'You should, you know.'

Yes, he knew but these days he never seemed to have the time and, anyway, he and Natalie always got together for birthdays and things like that. Birthdays, yipes! What was the date, what was the sodding date? Chrissy would know. Yes, of course she bloody would, it was her birthday he was trying to remember.

'Anything been, er, happening recently?' Jack inquired as innocently as possible.

'Like what?'

'Oh, you know, been to any good parties or whatever?'

'You mean like, um, birthday parties?'

'All right, I admit it. When is it then?'

'Tomorrow. So you'd better get your skates on.'

Her crooked teeth and snub nose made her look like a Dickensian street urchin who'd been cleaned up and let loose in Miss Selfridge. Of all the people he knew, Chrissy was the hardest to buy presents for. Being a deejay, she never needed records or concert tickets, things that Jack could easily lay his hands on. Her amazing inventiveness when choosing gifts for others demanded a similar amount of thought in return. Last year he happened to mention an interest in pool and she bought him a two piece, chestnut and gold cue in a monogrammed case. The Roebuck was hardly the place for such a classy piece of equipment but Jack cherished it and polished the wood every week. One day he'd have a custom-built blue baize table to go with it.

'I'd better go soon.' Chrissy began getting herself together.

'I'll get that book I promised to lend you,' said Jack.

Cardboard boxes, piled high with junk, surrounded Jack's mattress and he tipped one of them out onto the bed. In amongst the debris he found a dog-eared paperback. It was all about a woman who took an hallucinogenic drug so powerful that her dreams became a reality for anyone who was in them. Somehow, Jack knew that would appeal to Chrissy and he hoped the tacky, irrelevant cover illustration didn't put her off too much.

'If you like it, I'll get you some more of his stuff.'

Chrissy regarded the book suspiciously. 'It's not all about some berk floating around in space is it? You know I don't like that sort of thing.'

'No, it's nothing like that. Believe me.'

Flicking to page one Chrissy scanned it rapidly and turned over. Jack watched in silence. She was an avid reader, much more so than he, and got through two or three books a week. At the end of the first chapter she looked up and caught Jack with a superior looking smile on his face.

Jack flicked to the TV section in the paper as Chrissy let herself out. Nothing on unless you happened to be forty-five, female and heavily into valium. Housewives' bloody choice. Hmmm, that was a good title for a song, housewives' choice, yeah.

Jack began scribbling on the back of a brown envelope. *Wherever you go it's a housewives' choice, 'cos the silent majority have no voice, they just bow to the man in the big Rolls-Royce, so wherever you go it's a housewives' choice.* If Otto was up to it, they could work out a few chords later on tonight and have it ready for tomorrow's rehearsal. Maybe they could score some sulphate at the Roebuck to get themselves in the mood. There was nothing like writing on speed, Jack's jaw tightened with anticipation. Just one year ago he had been totally green about drugs, thinking that pot was something you injected and taking heroin meant instantaneous death. Personally, smack was still out of bounds as far as he was concerned but he'd seen other people do it – hell, even Otto had a blast every now and again. Sure there were junkies and casualties just like there were crazy assholes who broke the speed limit, only being hit by a car was a lot more likely to happen to most people than OD'ing on skag.

Jack mused on this for a while and decided to roll a spliff. Running his tongue along the edge of a Silk Cut he peeled back the wet strip of paper and emptied the contents onto the low coffee table. Lighting a match, he held it under the small brown lump of hash until it crumbled softly between his thumb and forefinger. He sprinkled the powdered hash into the tobacco and mixed the two together thoroughly. A few sheets of Rizla

6

Kingsize lay loose beside what was left of their packet. He took one and swept the mixture off the table and into it. Making sure that one end was fatter, he began to roll from the thin end until he had a large white cone. He ripped another piece out of the decimated cardboard packet and made a small roach which he popped into the thin end of the joint. Finally he twisted the paper at the other end into a short fuse and then bit it off, leaving a tiny aperture. Putting the joint to his lips, he sucked air through it and nodded approvingly. Not too tight and not too loose, just right. It seemed a shame to consume such a well-made object but it wasn't gonna do much good unlit. As he pulled on the lighted spliff, the hot smoke burned the back of his throat harshly.

'Ahhhh . . .' he breathed and thick white jets billowed forth from his nostrils and mouth.

Jack was rifling through Grace's room, when the doorbell rang. Somewhere amongst all the hairsprays, compacts and tampons there was a small white tin with the word 'Hello' written on it in gold. Inside, there were a number of sky blue pills speckled with navy spots and . . . ahhh . . . the odd one or two wouldn't be missed. Jack placed one on his tongue, shuddered at the rusty, bitter taste and flipped it down his throat.

The large oak front door was fitted with an all-seeing eye and Jack had become accustomed to using it before answering. Standing a few feet away from the door, Andy's gangly frame looked abnormally squat through the distorting fish-eye lens. He seemed unaware that he was being watched and scratched his balls.

With hair cut so short he was nearly bald, Andy looked mean and violent in a way that didn't connect with the cute, carrot-topped kid who always got away with murder. This guy couldn't get away with crossing the road at a zebra. For several minutes Jack waited, hoping that Andy would suddenly think of something better to do. Instead of ringing the bell again, Andy remained where he was, in full view of the seeing eye and Jack became aware that it was he who was being watched. Tiptoeing away down the hall he turned and marched noisily back to the door.

'You were there all the time, weren't ya?' Andy beamed.

Jack froze in the doorway. Shaking hands would be too formal, they were old mates, but hugging was out of the question.

'I saw your shadow under the door.'

Trust him to spot that, Hammersmith's answer to bloody Raffles.

'Yeah, well, can't be too careful these days,' Jack admitted reluctantly.

When they were both eleven, Andy had broken into Jack's parents' caravan the night before the whole Shaw family were due to go on holiday. Granny nearly had a heart attack when, five miles outside Bognor Regis, she went to investigate the peculiar smell and found Andy hiding in the picnic hamper. He hadn't dared to come out, even to go to the toilet. When Mr Mason finally answered his telephone at around midnight he was incoherent with alcohol and Natalie decided a fortnight away might do Andy a bit of good.

'Tasty, really tasty.' Andy marvelled at the high ceiling as they strolled down the long hall. 'Live 'ere on your own do ya?'

'You must be joking, not for seventy-five quid a week, nah there's three of us. Me, Otto, the guitarist in the group, and his bird.'

Andy's eyebrow twitched almost imperceptibly.

'What did you get done for?' asked Jack as he led the way into the living room and flopped into one of the brightly coloured beanbags.

Andy hovered awkwardly.

'Sit down, it's only a beanbag, it won't bite you.'

'I 'it this bird, didn' I.' Shifting about in the bag, Andy gradually made himself comfortable. 'WPC somefin' or uvver.'

Jack sniggered, there was no point in denying the man had a certain style.

'Concussion I give 'er, took free of 'em to pull me off of 'er and then, bing-bing, six monfs. They said I was lucky, coulda been prison,' he grinned cheekily.

Jack's brain suddenly cranked into top gear as the blue started to come on. His armpits began to sweat and he felt his balls writhe and shrink.

8

'Fancy a smoke?' Something to calm down.

''S all right, got me own. It's important to 'ave your own.' Andy produced a small pouch of tobacco, and proceeded to roll the thinnest excuse for a cigarette that Jack had ever seen.

Reaching over to the low, black coffee table he grabbed a wooden cigar box and opened it. Andy's eyes widened as Jack took out a huge cone-shaped spliff and lit it.

'Oh yeah, I see what you mean, right.' Andy put down his snout, accepted the joint and began taking shallow puffs.

'No, no, like this.' Air whistled through Jack's teeth as he filled his lungs. 'Then hold it,' he hissed, 'until you feel it's gone right down to your stomach and then . . .' Slowly he exhaled. 'Try that a few times while I sort out some sounds.'

A rhythm guitar scratched out several beats and then bounced away in a flurry of echo repeats, a bass drum boomed like a depth charge and an out of tune piano clanked oddly behind the beat. Abruptly, the music stopped and the sound of voices, arguing in Jamaican patois, span dizzily in a sea of reverb.

'Riddim farward,' one of them barked and a metallic drum roll rang out like the bell on an old fire engine. The music stuttered into action again. Jack's mind waded dreamily in amongst the sounds. Organ stabs shot past like comets and the bass line undulated like a fat rubber wave.

'I remember it was you who first got me into reggae an' dub an' that, I used to hate it,' Jack grunted with amusement. 'And James Brown, you used to love him.'

'I got souuulllll,' Andy screeched. 'Huh! And I'm sssuperbad. Eeeeyyyoww! 'Ow's your group gettin' on? 'Eard you 'ad a single out not long ago.'

'It's still out. We've sold about five thousand so far. It's weird you know 'cos, when you think of five thousand separate human beings all buying the same piece of music, it seems like loads, but it's not even enough to scrape the top hundred, not without airplay.'

Asking Chrissy had been the last resort and a pretty far fetched idea at that, considering her mainstream pop/oldies format. The record company pluggers had come up against a solid wall of lack of interest from the radio producers and deejays who baulked at the idea of yet another punk band. The flood-gates were already wide open and the media vampires were looking for something new to get their teeth into.

'We got a couple of great reviews, wanna see 'em?' Jack hurried off to his room and came back moments later with a large scrapbook. 'This is from the *NME*.' He pointed to a single column.

Silently mouthing the words, Andy ran his finger carefully over the print. When he came to the end, he frowned and went back to the beginning.

'Good bit about me, isn't it?'

'Which bit?'

'Where it says "powerhouse drumming", that bit.'

'Oh yeah, yeah. But 'oo's this Bertolt geezer?'

Jack had been wondering about that himself.

'All of which should make Bertolt a very happy . . . mensch, is it? Wassat?'

'Search me. Good though isn't it?' Re-lighting the spliff, Jack inhaled deeply and closed his eyes. The inside of his lids scratched roughly against his bloodshot eyeballs and a thin film of tears formed to moisten the friction.

'Anuvver one already?' Andy's eyes were scarlet.

'Same spliff, different dimension,' Jack observed profoundly. They both began to laugh.

Soon they were rolling around on the floor unable to speak or even catch their breath. 'I-i-it's good innit?' Jack stuttered and then doubled over, howling like a hyena. Clutching his stomach with both hands, Andy staggered to his feet.

'I fink I'm gonna-huh-huh-piss meself,' he gurgled and charged out of the room.

When he returned Jack had calmed down considerably. 'Listen, I've got to shoot off to rehearsal. What's the time, any idea?'

The chunky black and gold digital watch looked very chic and quite at odds with Andy's functional skinhead uniform.

'Nearly noon. Whereabouts are you goin'?'

'Fulham Broadway.'

'Aaaaayyyy!'

Of course, Andy lived just a few blocks away in Churchill Court. Jack had been there once or twice but Mr Mason was a sour, unpleasant bastard whose capacity for booze knew no bounds. The flat constantly stank of piss and whenever Jack visited he used to breathe only through his mouth and hope that no one would notice. There was an older brother as well, not the brightest of men, with a temper so vicious he made the father seem like Snow White.

The bus pulled away from the Army & Navy and headed down Victoria Street towards the train station. They sat in the front seat on the top deck, the only way to travel. From here you could see everything, from the secretaries hard at work on the fourth floor of their office building down to the well-camouflaged bald patch on top of the middle-aged businessman's head as he prepared to take an early train home.

"'S been a long time since I was 'ere last,' Andy observed nostalgically.

The site of their old school lay half a mile south in Pimlico and the memories of bunking off and hanging around the station came flooding back.

'Do you remember 'ow we used to ponce money off the commuters?'

How could Jack forget Andy's brilliantly flawless scheme of simply asking passers-by for money? It was crazy but it worked, the only snag being that it was also mind-bogglingly boring. In those days it was hard to think of something to spend the money on so they frittered it away on crap like disposable cigarette lighters or matching pen and pencil sets. If they had kept all that money think how much sulphate they could buy now. Grammes and grammes of the stuff, enough to fill a bath.

Jack's ears roared with blood as the blue gave him another rush and the muffled hum of combined traffic suddenly became distinct, individual sounds. The soothing purr of a black cab overtaking on the right, the guttural, choking throb of an old BSA motorcycle revving impatiently at the lights, a pram wheel, badly in need of oil, squeaking over the pedestrian crossing.

As the bus turned out of Buckingham Palace Road and into Pimlico Road, Andy pointed to a gutted mansion block on the corner. 'D'you remember them?'

Bunking off from school they had decided to hole up in the disused block of flats for a quiet smoke, tobacco only in those days, and lo and behold who should appear but the filth. Three pandas and a meat-wagon, all with sirens blaring, surrounded the building and a scratchy megaphone voice asked them to come out and no one would get hurt. The pigs were pretty fucking angry when they realised that the Starsky and Hutch histrionics were all for a couple of kids, but they brightened up at the discovery of Andy's burgeoning criminal record.

When the case came to court, after a delay of some weeks due to one of the arresting officers' skiing accident, they were fitted up. The police quoted the boys as admitting their guilt to a charge of attempted burglary. Apparently they were supposed to be nicking lead off the roof, though neither would have recognised a piece of lead if it fell on them. So began Andy's first stretch in approved school. With a clean sheet and reasonable grades, Jack got off with a recommendation to see the school psychiatrist once a week.

At the top of Pimlico Road the bus turned into Lower Sloane Street, crossing an invisible boundary between Jack's old world and his new one. A sparse, tasteful antique shop nestled comfortably next to the austere facade of a private men's club. A row of terraced houses sat back from the pavement with huge bay windows and stone balconies full of potted plants looking a deep, mournful green in the dim November light.

Andy's stomach grumbled with quiet thunder. 'I'm starvin'. I don't understand it though, I 'ad a massive breakfast.' His belly groaned again.

'It's just the munchies that's all. That gold Leb's a real demon.' Putting his hand in his shirt pocket Jack fished out the other blue he'd stolen from Grace's room. 'Here, this should take the edge off your appetite.'

Andy swallowed the pill. 'Gordon Bennett,' he screwed up his face, 'tastes like earwax. What's it do?'

'By the time we hit World's End, you'll know the answer to that.'

Even on a grim day like this, Sloane Square was buzzing. A handful of punks sat around the fountain on the square itself, posing for the traffic as it whizzed past. A gang of blond-haired tourists in Union Jack bowler hats gawped at them, not realising who looked the more ridiculous. Chic expensive-looking women weaved in and out of Peter Jones, some carrying recently purchased goods, others had the chauffeur do it for them. The bus throttled down the King's Road and stopped outside Boy with its dazzling display of fluorescent clothes.

'Punks,' sneered Andy, 'I 'ate 'em.'

'Oi, oi, what do you think these are?' Jack demanded, tapping the thigh of his black, zip covered trousers.

'Yeah, well I don't include you wiv the rest of them. I mean, look at the state of that.'

A girl with a tangled shock of Krazy Koloured hair stood just inside the shop doorway wearing a black plastic bin liner, fingerless fishnet gloves and matching stockings. A thin silver chain connected her pierced right earlobe to its corresponding nostril.

'I'd like to rip that chain right out of 'er fucking nose.'

Letting out a sigh of resignation, Jack looked the girl over once more. She was gorgeous.

'Okay. One, two, one two three four.'

Jack battered the snare drum in a short burst of machine-gun fire and the band thrashed into 'We Don't Need You'. This was the only number in the fifteen-minute set whose tempo never varied because Jack simply counted it in as fast as it was possible for him to play. His right hand was a blur as it pounded, eight to the bar, on the sizzling cymbal and his right ankle was stiff and fatigued from kicking relentlessly on the bass drum pedal. Boom-tack-boom-boom-tack-boom-tack-boom-boom-tack. Salty sweat poured down his forehead and into his eyes, stinging them sharply. The thick wooden drumsticks began to slip out of his moist hands and he gripped them more tightly. His fingers locked with cramp and he tried to relax his grip, but couldn't. Flailing at the drum kit in a spastic fashion. Splinters began to fly from the sticks as they were bashed against the hard metal rim of the drums. The tempo slowed fractionally and Jack's heart pounded in the back of his throat as he pushed the rhythm back up to its original speed. The blue worked its magic once more and he began to fly, his arms and legs pumped manically and he felt his mind leave his body momentarily. The cramp eased up, his movements became fluid once more and he thundered around the three tom-toms in a spontaneous burst of improvisation. Glancing over to Otto he saw the guitarist's sly, hooded eyes soften with admiration. As the song came to a close, Jack's bare torso was covered in a glistening sheen. The room rang with silence.

The guitar amplifier crackled at Otto unhooked his strap and leaned the instrument against the wall. Lighting a cigarette he turned to face the rest of the group. 'It's a pity we didn't play it like that on the record.'

Unofficially, he was the leader of The Destroyers, mainly because of the quiet but firm manner which enabled him to get his own way without seeming pushy. He'd managed to get the group a steady stream of gigs and a recording contract without the aid of a manager or an agent. Listening to him hustle on the telephone was a real joy, as he came out with lines like, 'Yes of course I understand your anti-punk policy but please, don't be fooled by the name, actually we're a string quartet' and 'He's still in a meeting? Well, could you ask him to call back as soon as possible, it is rather urgent. Certainly, it's Dr Davis at St Stephen's Hospital –'. That particular one had yet to fail, the peculiar thing being that the victims always took the hoax in good humour. When it came to women, however, his gift of the gab beat a hasty retreat. That was where Jack came in and returned the favour with his own special brand of chat. By telling the blatant truth, 'See that guy over there? Yeah? Well, he's the son of a millionaire, and he's got a beautiful motor outside waiting to whisk the four of us off to an urban paradise,' the mission would invariably be accomplished. Perhaps the word 'millionaire' was a slight exaggeration, Otto's mother was some sort of Scandinavian baroness, but it was probably the word that caught most people's attention. The real pushovers were the Sloane Rangers who came down to the shabbier end of the King's Road, to the Roebuck, for a slice of real life and the obligatory bit of rough. But not too rough. The combination of Jack and Otto worked a charm.

Jack drew on the spliff and offered it to Anne who took it greedily. There was something very masculine about their lead singer, the way she smoked, walked and talked, or rather didn't. Suspicions of lesbianism were voiced the moment she'd left the audition but this was 1977 so who cared? The only problem she posed for Jack was that he desperately wanted to get into her pants and the constant exposure to her highly individual sex appeal made life all the more difficult. Five nights a week they rehearsed in a room so tiny he could almost taste her. Out of town gigs were even more frustrating: as they couldn't afford hotels, the group would huddle together under a blanket in the back of the van. Anne snored divinely. In the universities and the more up-market clubs there would often be two dressing rooms but Anne waived her privilege as a woman and changed with the rest of the group, thereby enabling Jack to paint a vivid mental picture of her while masturbating. Knowing he could rely on his buddy's discretion, he had revealed his passion for Anne to Otto and had received a typical piece of advice. 'Why tell me? Tell her.' The thought of continuing to work with someone who'd refused his advances was anathema to Jack. So that was out of the question. Running into various old flames in the Roebuck was bad enough. If it weren't for the fact that they were a punk band, he could have written her a love song lyric to sing and hoped that she got the message. But there was no room for that kind of 'moon in June' crap in their repertoire. Just honest to goodness rage at the government, the church and all those other fascist pinheads. Abuse of power comes as no surprise, that kind of thing.

'Oh, by the way, I've got a new set of words.' Jack produced the tattered envelope and passed it to Anne. 'If you like them, Otto and I can start work on them tonight.' Leaning over her broad shoulder Jack re-read the lyrics. 'What do you think?'

Anne nodded sagely and handed them back.

'Let's have a look.' Unstrapping his bass guitar, Alex held out his hand. His conventional Afro hair style and chubby West Indian features were completely at odds with the standard punk look of pasty anorexia.

Had Alex been white, Jack would have insisted on him doing something about his hair at least, but somehow the idea of asking a black man to alter his appearance seemed incredibly insulting. Plus, he was an ace bassie, master of the reggae one-drop style and a real pleasure to jam with. Bit by bit, Alex was sneaking in more adventurous bass lines, making the music less frenetic and more melodic. He'd probably be a lot happier in a straightforward reggae band but his beige complexion and strong South London accent had not found favour with the local, heavy militant Rastas. So he had to cast his net a little wider. After answering an ad in the *Melody Maker* he turned up at the audition and blew their heads off. Though punk and reggae were the only styles acceptable within The Destroyers' format, Alex was, in fact, a closet jazz-rocker. He had once read an interview with Jaco Pastorius, generally accepted as the king of bass players, who stated that endless practice and a refusal to listen to any other bassists had helped him achieve his current status. So, when Alex wasn't rehearsing or performing with the group, he practised. Endlessly. Jack couldn't remember a single conversation they'd had that wasn't music related and as Alex didn't smoke or drink he was even excluded from the stoned verbal meanderings that the rest of the group indulged in. During interviews, Anne was consistently singled out for questioning, but journalists soon found out they were on a hiding to nothing and turned their attentions to Otto and Jack. Invariably, Alex would stare out of the window, occasionally confirming a statement made by one of the others. Like John Entwistle and Bill Wyman before him, Alex was a rock. Strangely enough, Anne seemed to have more time for him than for anyone else.

Otto stubbed out his half-finished cigarette and took a deep breath. Normally he would smoke it right down to the filter and, to prove it, he had orange stains permanently ingrained into the tip of his right thumb and forefinger. Something was wrong.

'Anyone who isn't sitting, better do so.'

Jack returned to his position behind the drum kit while the others arranged themselves, cross-legged, on the floor.

'I've been talking to the powers that be,' he began, 'and I'm afraid we've got a problem.'

A look of concern spread across all three faces and Alex began twirling his hair around his little finger anxiously.

'Obviously if the single had done well then none of this would've come up but . . .' He searched for the appropriate words.

Jack's mind darted from pillar to post trying to ignore the inevitable. It was the lyrics, he was sure of it. Hadn't he insisted Otto strike a deal with an independent label to avoid any commercial compromises? And here they were, five minutes after signing a major recording contract, being told to soften up or ship out. They should have realised that no self-respecting businessman was going to shell out good money just to hear four young upstarts tell him he's a moral vacuum. Abuse of power comes as no bloody surprise at all.

'What's the problem?'

Jack jumped a little at the sound of Anne's breathy contralto.

Staring at the patch of grey carpet between his feet, Otto cleared his throat.

Christ, it was worse than Jack had imagined. Someone was about to get the push. The tension was almost palpable. He and Otto were buddies, there was no way Otto would've waited until now to tell him he was fired. But Alex, well, his image was less than perfect and record companies were notoriously ignorant of their artists' ability to play their instruments. The more sinister implication was that of racism and Jack suddenly became aware that he would not tolerate this at all. Whatever reasons they gave for wanting Alex out it would boil down to the same thing. If the company didn't want the band, as they were, then they wouldn't have them at all. A half smile played on his lips and his eyes misted over in angry defiance.

'Anne?' whispered Otto.

Jack's heart stopped. The blue rushed again and his face froze in astonishment as Otto and Anne gazed, unblinkingly, at each other.

'I had a feeling,' she said hoarsely. 'What is it exactly?'

'We have to find a new singer. Period.' Otto sliced at the air with a firm karate chop.

'No,' said Jack loudly and the others looked up.

Otto sighed dejectedly. 'We have no choice. If we don't co-operate they'll sit on us. No more records, no chance of getting another deal, nothing.'

'Unless we get out there on tour and prove to those bastards that people wanna see us. As we are. If they come to a gig and see five hundred kids going apeshit to our stuff then –'

'Otto's right,' said Anne.

How could anyone resist that voice? It was like sandpaper on velvet.

'Without the support of the company you couldn't afford to play anywhere.'

Already she was saying 'you' instead of 'we'.

'That's rubbish. Look, we've –'

'Jack, Jack please.' Otto waved him down. 'You don't know enough about it to have an opinion. The kind of places we play don't pay enough to cover the cost of the PA half the time.'

'Oh yeah? Well why the hell did you wait until the end of the rehearsal to say all this? I mean it's not exactly perfect timing is it?'

'You're right. It was stupid. I just thought that – I don't know, I just thought . . .'

'It's okay,' Anne smiled. 'Really, it was a nice thought.' She stood up and walked over to him. They hugged each other and Otto dug his chin deep into her shoulder.

'Alex.' She held out her hand and pulled the bassist to his feet. Gently she drew him to her and caressed the back of his neck. Eventually they relaxed their embrace and she stepped in front of the drum kit.

Taking her extended hand, Jack kissed it lightly and all at once she began to cry.

'I may as well tell you now,' Jack croaked, 'I always fancied the hell out of you.'

The tears streamed down her face as Anne gathered her things in silence. The ever-present red notebook, the spare T-shirt draped over the microphone stand and, lastly, the microphone itself, were each packed carefully into a khaki hold-all. Opening the sound-proofed double doors she turned to look at Jack.

'Yeah, me too.'

At four o'clock the sky was dark, the atmosphere close and damp. Otto and Jack sat in the stationary Citroën.

'What are we going to do?' asked Jack as Otto switched on the ignition and the car choked to life.

'Find a new singer I suppose. Is anyone coming?'

Leaning out of his window, Jack looked back along the row of parked cars. 'You're okay,' he affirmed and they eased into the road.

'Do you want to find something good on the radio?' Otto nodded toward the dashboard.

'Could we leave it for a while?'

'Sure.' Stamping on the accelerator Otto looked straight ahead and began to whistle.

'I loved her you know?' Jack's voice trembled with exasperation.

'So you told me.'

'And now – I mean I couldn't look her in the eye again. Did you hear what she said to me?'

'Yup.'

'I can't get over it.' Jack shook his head in disbelief.

After a few minutes he switched the radio on. *Got to keep on dancin', keep on dancin', got to keep on dancin', keep on dancin'.* The multi-tracked male voices broke into harmony, forming a loathsome, saccharine chord. 'Christ, this disco crap makes me want to puke. Those fucking endless bass drum fours, boom boom boom boom boom boom boom boom, drives me nuts!' He punched the tuning buttons and was treated to Kenneth Williams whining nasally on 4, some long-haired classical shit on 3 and MOR swing on 2.

'Leave that on, it's Sarah Vaughan,' said Otto eagerly. It was his car after all, dammit. The song finished and was replaced by a syrupy string arrangement of a familiar TV theme. 'Okay, you can kill it now. What about Chrissy's show?'

'Finishes at three.'

They drove home in silence.

Two

He was like a wiry mountain lion with prominent cheekbones and a gaunt, hollow face covered in three-day-old stubble. A shaggy, black mane swept back from his head, revealing an exaggerated widow's peak, and then cascaded half-way down his back. The ever-present leather jacket was scuffed with age, perfectly complementing its owner. Sunken eyes lurked mysteriously behind impenetrable sunglasses and an unlit cigarette dangled at an angle from his mouth.

Chrissy gazed about the nightclub with mild disdain. Welcome to the pleasure dome, with its elitist admission policy, overpriced drinks and out-of-date music. Rock stars, film stars and every two-bit hanger-on who managed to slime their way past the bouncers. Chrissy's escort was none other than Richard Keyes, guitarist and backbone of the world's most notorious rock 'n' roll band. They were the reason she'd decided to become a disc jockey at the age of twenty-two when their debut record was released. All the major radio stations refused to play it because of the 'subversive' lyrics. The first drug bust, coupled with Keyes's alleged paedophilia, hadn't done the record sales any harm either. The group were lionised by those who felt the establishment needed a violent shake up. Now, of course, they had been absorbed into the existing power structure like every other successful artist who initially wages war against it. Once Chrissy would have considered chopping off a finger in exchange for this time with Keyes but now all she wanted to do was get rid of him.

The live interview that morning had been fun. Keyes was stoned and at first it seemed as though he might not make it through the hour. Then came the first commercial break and off he went to the bathroom. It wasn't difficult to deduce what he'd been doing in there because, when the interview resumed, his sardonic wit sparkled and shone as wickedly as it had done back in 1964. There were five commercial breaks altogether and during every one Keyes went to the bathroom for some powdered inspiration. It was when he came back the final time with white flecks dotted around his runny nostrils that Chrissy began to question her original motive in asking for the interview. Maybe he wouldn't make a suitable father for her baby after all.

She was thirty-five years old. There was no getting away from it. Thirty-five and childless. Being a spinster (what a horrible word) had caused several rumours to circulate but her friends remained loyal and everyone else could take a flying leap. But motherhood . . . well that was something else. Chrissy had waited patiently for the right man to walk into her life but now time was running out. God was obviously male.

'Okay, darlin' you ready to leave?'

Yes, she was, but not with him.

'Your place or mine, hyerk! hyerk!'

What a disgusting laugh. It sounded like someone unblocking a drain. 'I'm sorry I have a splitting headache. I'm going home.'

She knew Keyes wouldn't waste five minutes before chatting up another 'skirt' and in a few hours Chrissy's name would vanish forever from his memory. She slung her handbag over a tired shoulder and walked out of the club. Outside she hailed a taxi. The cab sped along Piccadilly and through Knightsbridge. Neon signs blurred into one another like a slowly exposed photograph and Chrissy's mind drifted. Suddenly she was thrown sideways.

'Fuckin' roads,' the driver swore. 'It's the bloody GLC, you know, they don't know their arse from their elbow.' The cab bounced and groaned in agreement. 'And where does the rate-payer's money go? I'll tell you where it bloody goes –' The question was purely rhetorical and Chrissy wasn't listening anyway.

This back street seemed familiar. 'Driver, would you pull over please?'

The cabby was still bemoaning the price of shock absorbers as the cab lurched off down the street leaving Chrissy on the pavement. Now was it number thirty-one or thirty-three? She'd always had trouble remembering the address. Standing in front of the two adjacent doors she recognised the brown one on the left. It was very late to be calling unexpectedly on someone she hadn't seen for two years.

'Christine, is that you? Please – please do come in. It's wonderful to see you. How've you been keeping? The flat's in a bit of a mess but – isn't it strange only yesterday your name came up in conversation and –'

'Oh?'

'– yes and now here you are.' Martin's arms gesticulated wildly to emphasise just how amazing it really was. Behind his small, round, wire-framed spectacles lay all the innocence of a new-born baby.

The flat was spotless. Glass and metal gleamed from every direction. Martin ushered Chrissy into the living room and onto a shiny black sofa. Her own place hadn't been this clean since the disastrous two weeks in '71 when Phyllis came to stay. Her mother had hated it when Chrissy started calling her Phyllis. 'I'm Mummy, darling. Please don't call me that name.' That name. Sometimes it was hard to believe they were related at all. Phyllis had more problems than the entire cast of *Crossroads* with enough prescribed pills in her bathroom cabinet to start a pharmacy.

Martin hovered. 'It hasn't changed that much since you were last here. How's the music business? Seen any good bands lately? Actually a friend of mine is playing at the Half Moon tomorrow, perhaps you'd –'

'Sorry, I'm busy tomorrow.'

'No it's my fault. People must pester you constantly.'

True enough and not surprising either since Chrissy's show

had an audience of four and a half million. 'What have you been up to?' she asked.

'Oh, you know, the usual.'

Martin was bar manager at the hotel in which they had first met. Chrissy had been invited to lunch by the director of a large record company. 'This isn't what I asked for at all,' he'd bellowed, 'take it back and bring me what I ordered.' Martin was easily flustered and she'd felt sorry for him right away. 'I'm sorry, sir,' he offered meekly, 'what was it again?' 'I asked,' the fat-cat drawled pedantically, 'for an eight-ounce steak. What we have here is a small turd burnt to a crisp.' The regular waiter had been ill that day and Martin was doing his best to cope. 'Take it back!' the fat-cat boomed again. Several other customers turned their heads to see what all the fuss was in aid of. Martin's cheeks glowed a purple mixture of anger and embarrassment. 'If you could wait one –' 'I'm going to ask you for the last time to get rid of it. Now!' The fat-cat grinned facetiously at Chrissy and she wanted to spit. Martin's hands shook with subdued fury as he lifted the offending plate from the table, and knocked Chrissy's orange juice into her lap. 'Well don't just stand there gawking, get her a towel.' 'No, no. I'm all right really.' The sensation of ice cold liquid seeping into her jeans was highly unpleasant but Martin was on the verge of tears.

She had almost forgotten the incident when, back at the same hotel a few weeks later, Martin appeared at her table, apologising for his previous incompetence. Somehow he managed to turn the apology into an offer of dinner and they spent a lovely evening watching Martin's video collection of old American pop shows. They continued to see each other regularly for a month and then, as always, sex reared its ugly head. In the back row of a seedy cinema he made a pass at her. It failed miserably.

'Whoops! That must be Larry.' Martin went to answer a knock at the front door.

Larry? The name didn't ring any bells.

'Hellooo how ahhhhre you. Mmmmmmwuh! Mmmmmm-whuh!'

Whoever Larry was, butch he certainly wasn't.

'Oooooh I hope I'm not disturbing anything.' A tall, thin, bearded man, wearing an exquisitely tailored pin-striped suit, sauntered into the room.

'No, not at all. This is Chrissy, an old friend. Chrissy this is –'

'Larry, yes, hello.' His hand flopped limply into hers as though she was expected to kiss it and curtsy. 'Don't I know you from somewhere?' his nasal tone mocked as he slumped down beside her. 'Wait a minute, you're – don't tell me – you're um . . .'

'Chrissy has her own radio show on LWS.'

'Yes of course. How silly of me. You see I don't really listen to the radio.'

Chrissy stiffened slightly. 'What do you do?'

'Me? Oh a little bit of this, a little bit of that, you know.'

'No, I don't.'

'Larry's a financial adviser. He puts together business deals.'

'Ahh. A middle man.' Chrissy's tone had become equally mocking. Though she hadn't admitted it to herself, Martin was a sort of last resort. Larry, however, was making it crystal clear he wasn't about to leave. She wondered what, exactly, their relationship consisted of and arrived at a disappointing conclusion. 'I've changed my mind about tomorrow. I'd love to come to the Half Moon with you.'

Martin's eyes lit up and then glanced nervously at Larry who was absent-mindedly flicking through a magazine.

'I'll call you tomorrow and confirm.' Chrissy got up and moved towards the door.

Larry looked up. 'Leaving so soon? Oh I am sorry.'

A tall, dark and, to complete the cliché, rather handsome man regarded the female forms in various states of undress as the escalator trundled down to the underground. For no apparent reason he turned and looked up at Chrissy. Spot the difference, huh? An old Indian couple stood on the platform looking cold and out of place in their ill-fitting Western apparel. Wind from the mouth of the tunnel announced that a train was approaching and a few moments later it thundered into the station. The brown-eyed handsome man walked deliberately along to a smoking carriage and Chrissy followed. He sat down in one of the seats marked for elderly or handicapped passengers. There didn't seem to be anything wrong with him so Chrissy sat opposite, hoping that he wouldn't think there was something the matter with her. He smiled. Hot blood boiled in her cheeks and she began reading an advertisement for a temping agency directly above him. She hadn't even managed to smile back, God, how embarrassing. No need to take the Lord's name in vain, come on now, Chrissy, pull yourself together. The doors hissed shut and the train pulled away from the platform and into the tunnel. Fishing a pack of smokes out of his jacket pocket, the brown-eyed handsome man lit up. He drew hard on the cigarette and held the smoke in his lungs for a long time before breathing out. Their eyes met.

'Want one?' he offered.

'Uh, no thanks. I don't smoke.' Jesus my beads, what a stupid thing to say.

'You don't mind if I do?'

'No, go ahead. It's your privilege.' She'd managed to make that sound as though she was head of the Cancer Research Fund.

'It's a filthy habit, I know. I suppose I just haven't the will power.'

The way he pulled on that Camel indicated that he was a sixty-a-day man. Though Chrissy had never quite reached that stage, giving up had been torture. First, she put on a stone and a half and then there were two solid months of coughing up puce-coloured phlegm. And Phyllis, bless her, was wholly to blame. 'And if you're a good girl, you can have one of Mummy's fags.' It was hardly suitable bribery for a fourteen-year-old.

'I – I found it very difficult to give up.'

'Really?' said the brown-eyed handsome man. 'How did you do it? I've tried everything, literally everything. Nicotine-flavoured chewing gum, herbal cigarettes, attachable tar filters, you know, those horrible little plastic things that turn yellow and are supposed to put you off smoking for life. How'd you manage it?'

26

'I just stopped,' said Chrissy matter-of-factly. And so did the conversation.

The tube station at Parson's Green was deserted. Chrissy walked along the platform, perilously close to the warning white stripe at the edge. One slip and it would all be over. No, things were not that bad. But the possibility was always there, like a secret trap-door in the cell of solitary confinement. Perhaps tomorrow, perhaps never. At least there was choice.

The chip shop on Parson's Green Lane was open and, as she had no wish to tackle the washing-up back at the flat, Chrissy settled for pickled egg and chips. Becoming a vegetarian hadn't affected her life as radically as she thought it would. The main problem was remembering to warn dinner party hosts in case they were planning on serving rabbit risotto or something. Otherwise, the traditional meat and two veg dish was very easily censored. Whenever she admitted to being a herbivore, people would nod knowingly as though she fitted some sort of stereo-type. Mmm, the vinegar had soaked right into the chips making them deliciously soggy and Chrissy crammed another handful into her mouth.

The Ansafone tape contained just one message. Julia was taking yet another Exegesis course and wanted to know if Chrissy had changed her mind. The course consisted of being locked in a bare room with no food or bed for forty-eight hours. During that time a number of 'instructors' wandered in at various intervals and shouted insults at you. After this horrendous ordeal you returned to civilisation with renewed vigour and a strange feeling of relief. All this for only sixty-two pounds, excluding VAT. With acute nostalgia Chrissy looked back on the days when she and Julia had shared a flat.

'Oh you can't be serious,' Julia had crowed, when they'd been to every fashionable stall in Kensington Market and Chrissy now wanted to try Marks & Spencer. 'You'll end up looking like a Jewish grandmother.' Julia's own clothes bore more than a passing resemblance to those worn by the haggard prostitutes who hung around Earl's Court. It was no use, Chrissy wasn't allowed to leave the market until she had purchased something. 'What are those for?' She'd pointed to a display of miniature silver spoons and scales. 'Oh, Chris, you're so naive.' Eventually they found a second-hall stall selling flower print dresses, paisley shirts and wide kipper ties. 'That's more like it,' said Julia as Chrissy held a plain orange blouse up against herself. It could just as easily have come from Marks & Spencer.

But Julia's understanding of the 'it's not what you buy, it's where you buy it' syndrome had turned out to be very thorough. She now owned five of the stalls herself. With a flourishing business and a dependable boyfriend she decided the time was right to have a child. If it weren't for the fact that her own work was so fulfilling, Chrissy felt she could at least have wallowed in self-pity. As things stood, she wasn't even being allowed that luxury.

Sliding a tape into the video recorder, she sat back and pressed the remote control. The familiar strains of the *Coronation Street* theme sped up and slowed down as the tape gradually settled in. Nothing like other people's problems to take your mind off your own.

Nine hours later Chrissy sat naked at her own kitchen table munching a piece of dry toast. It was the only food she could face after a restless night punctuated by bouts of vomiting.

The kitchen was a mess. Week-old remains of spaghetti clung like tiny limpets to an enormous pile of unwashed dishes in the sink and the usual aroma of garlic and blue cheese was at its most pungent. How she had ever seen eye to eye with Martin on anything was a complete mystery.

'Dancing in the Street' by Martha and the Vandellas burst from the radio reminding her that she was already late for work.

'Morning, madam.' The LWS security guard gave his customary welcome.

'Hi Mack.'

As she approached the studio, Chrissy noticed the red light above the door. Uh oh, it was even later than she'd thought.

'Several Italian terrorists were arrested in Rome today. Official sources indicate that –' Jim waved hello through the glass partition and Chrissy hurriedly seated herself at the microphone. '– they may be the ones responsible for the kidnapping of Mr Arnold Coltrane the prominent American businessman. I'll be back with the full stories behind the headlines at one thirty. Until then it's over to you, Chrissy.'

This was the only time she truly enjoyed. Three hours of sharing her personal taste in music with millions of other people and though she couldn't see them she could feel them, as her light, airy voice broadcast into their homes, offices and factories. This time always passed much too quickly.

Jim sat opposite as they drank coffee together in the canteen. In a way, he was too obvious. Single, middle-aged, slim and incredibly easy-going, this morning being a typical example. Any other news reader would have been in a blind panic, faced with the prospect of filling in until the deejay arrived. Not so with Jim. The word 'zen' seemed specially invented to describe him.

'What are you doing the rest of the day?' he inquired.

Here was the perfect opportunity. 'Nothing much. You?'

'I have to meet my mother at Charing Cross. She's coming to stay for a couple of weeks.'

Oh wonderful. Just great.

After Jim had gone, Chrissy hung around the canteen for some time. Apart from a number of doddery old programme directors the only visible male stood serving behind the food counter. A ravishing boy with all the sex appeal of Brando and Dean combined. His surly mouth curled up at one corner when he discovered Chrissy staring at him. It was no good. A boy like that probably had to beat off female admirers with a stick. Glancing over again she saw he had already turned his attention to a leggy blonde from the typing pool. Chrissy's heart sank. It was as though she existed in a dimension separate from the rest of the world, dying a slow death that nobody else was aware of.

'I'm her sister,' the woman cried out. The detective slapped her hard across the cheek. 'I'm her mother,' the woman shrieked in agony as he slapped her even harder. 'I'm her sister *and* her mother,' the woman broke down and wept. This was her favourite scene in a film she'd seen at least five times. A few seats to her left an old man belched himself awake. Otherwise the place was empty. Where were the Jack Nicholsons when you needed them?

Three

The singer hissed and growled over a smoothly orchestrated jazz backdrop, reminiscent of a thousand film noir scores. A no-good gangland punk wanders the streets aimlessly, looking for an easy mark, preferably female. He finds her in a bar on 48th and Broadway drinking Chivas Regal like there was no tomorrow. First he comes on heavy with the cologne and flattery then, when she's hooked, he tells her that there's another broad he's been trying to get rid of but can't. The easy mark is touched by the punk's sincerity and vulnerability and says there's no rush, he must let the other broad down easy so as not to hurt her. Meanwhile, the punk is waiting for his uncle's firm to find a vacancy but his rent is due and his landlord is a bastard. After six months of paying somebody's rent as well as her own, the easy mark finally goes to visit the punk at his, hitherto out of bounds, Lower East Side apartment and guess who's with him? The easy mark asks the other broad to get out but the other broad ain't going nowhere. The punk says hey, hey let's talk it over and the truth hits the easy mark like a Sugar Ray Robinson uppercut. She reaches into her handbag and cocks the Derringer that's been hiding there all the time.

'What is this rubbish?' Jack waved a joint in the direction of the record player and a long piece of ash toppled into a conveniently placed cup of coffee.

Nobody in the room answered so Jack tried to attract their attention by singing along with the record in the wrong key. Grace had her head buried in a book, written by a woman no doubt. She lay on the bare parquet floor propped up by a large orange cushion. Her reading spectacles began to slide down her wide, flat nose and she pushed them back up again. Touching his own nose Jack felt the dip in the bridge that would house a pair of spectacles perfectly had he any need of them. Somehow they didn't look quite right on Grace who seemed to ooze African authenticity though she'd been born and bred in Peterborough. She was incredibly beautiful in the fashion maga-zine sense of the word but Jack found her ebony features totally unattractive. The brightly coloured beads in her braided hair made her head look like a packet of liquorice all-sorts.

'I agree with Jack, it's awful, erryaggh!' Grace shivered and poked out her tongue.

Damn it. The stupid cow just didn't understand anything. He and Otto argued all the time about music, in fact most things, but that was how their friendship worked. Jolly old banter, what? And as usual she had ruined it.

Rising stiffly from his chair at the high wooden dining table, Otto loped toward the stereo amplifier and faded the volume down before taking the needle off the record. Seizing the opportunity, Jack asked, for the umpteenth time, whether they'd mind listening to the single.

'Again?' Otto said with an exaggerated roll of his eyes.

'I'd like to,' Grace piped up.

We don't need you, we don't need you, we don't need you, any of you. Posing with an imaginary guitar, Jack began duck-walking across the room in time to the frenzied tempo.

'Elvis Presley, Mick Jagger, they're all dead now.' Jack thrashed his arm around like a rabid windmill, yelling at the top of his voice. 'This is what's alive, nothing else.' Ninety seconds later the needle clunked rhythmically against the run-out groove. 'And the bastards say it's too short for radio play. Wadda they know? There's more energy in those two minutes than there is on an entire Rod Stewart album,' he panted breathlessly.

'If that's all they're worried about, I mean if they like it anyway, couldn't you just make it a bit longer?' asked Grace.

Otto's lips quivered fractionally as Jack stared at her in absolute horror his teeth grinding audibly.

'I'm thinking of going to the Roebuck.' he growled quietly. 'Anyone care to join me?' He gazed meaningfully at Otto who had managed to get his mirth under control.

'I'm afraid –' Otto began.

'I'd like to,' Grace chipped in.

'I can't,' Otto finished. 'Mum's in town, we're having dinner.'

Grace's lips pulled back to reveal a dazzlingly white smile. 'Ready in a jiff,' she said and skipped off to her room.

Jack walked over to where Otto sat at the cluttered dining table and patted him on the shoulder. 'Why do you put up with it?'

'Oh come on, man, she just gets under your skin, not mine.'

'Yeah, but nine times out of ten –'

'I'm prête,' Grace giggled in the doorway.

Rain drizzled down from the cold, grey sky as they waited for a number eleven bus. At this time of night Victoria Street was a long, thin ghost town. At five p.m. the inhabitants disappeared back to their suburban bungalows, only to reappear at nine a.m. the next morning. In between those times the huge, faceless mountains of concrete and glass that lined both sides of the street lay dormant. The handful of shops, seemingly open with their teasing lights and displays, were not. Traffic hummed along to and from the West End but, like everything else in Victoria, it was just passing through. Here, on the bland borderline between Pimlico and St James's, life came to an abrupt halt. Several hundred yards away, McDonald's stood out like a Belisha beacon amongst the uniform greyness. Some of Jack's old school acquaintances worked at the fast food joint, making it highly embarrassing for him to go in. On the few occasions that he had, they all pretended not to recognise him and he did likewise, feeling lucky he wasn't in their shoes. Being in a band wasn't really work, it was more like having a paid hobby, but selling cheeseburgers didn't look like it was a bundle of laughs.

'Jack, why don't you like me?'

Taken aback, Jack fumbled for the right words.

'I – I do.' Yes, that seemed satisfactory, a simple affirmation.

'But you don't really, do you?'

'You're his girl, not mine, right? So whatever I say has nothing to do with him.'

Grace nodded, accepting the terms under which she was being allowed to know the truth.

'You're a nice person and I think you and Otto may have something good going there but personally, would I want you to be my girlfriend?' He paused briefly. 'No.'

Jack felt pleased with his skilful handling of the situation and it wasn't until they alighted at the bus stop on the corner of Beaufort Street that he realised she hadn't spoken a word to him since.

From outside, the Roebuck looked like any other pub. As they crossed the King's Road, Jack looked up to the first-floor window, the silhouette of a man holding a pool cue danced on the shade. Adjacent to the window, a huge, bronze-coloured bird stuck out from the wall on iron supports. Inside, the downstairs bar had a shambolic, front room atmosphere and a heavy emphasis on elderly patronage. Men and women with twenty or thirty good drinking years behind them, happy to spend another twenty or thirty, permanently sozzled. Chattering loudly about anything from world politics to ingrowing toenails. Jack walked to the back of the bar, through the connecting door and began climbing the short flight of stairs. Grace dawdled along behind him, neatly making sure he was first to the bar.

Wearing a UCLA sweatshirt, a stars and stripes baseball cap, smoking a Marlboro Light and guzzling a can of Colt 45, Nick, the barman, paraded his nationality unashamedly. The cigarettes were duty free goodies from his most recent mystery trip abroad. Four or five times a year he left the country and no one knew where he went or why.

'As we've sort of agreed that we're not really friends . . .' Jack thrust his hand into his trousers and scooped out some silver. '. . . I won't offer to buy you a drink. After all, we're not hypocrites are we?' Hypocrite was Jack's favourite word and he used it mercilessly with total disregard for its rather harsh and insulting quality.

'Jack, my Gahhhhd!' Nick chuckled deeply, his long, brown goatee beard wagging on the end of his chin. 'Here, have one on me.' Cracking a tube of Colt, he handed the foaming tin to Grace. Jack smiled at her, she hated beer.

'Who's in tonight?' he glanced around the room.

A couple of Road Hogs, the local Hell's Angels chapter, sat facing each other on the far window sill. Abruptly, one of them spat a yellow glob into the other's drink and cheered approvingly as his friend put the glass to his lips and drained it. Understandably, they seemed to have the entire left side of the room to themselves. At the other end of the room there were three pool tables, two in use, surrounded by chairs pushed back against the walls. Most of the chairs were occupied but the pale green light made it hard to see individual faces.

'The usual assholes. Oh yeah, and a few pathetic representatives of our once great nation.' Nick put his hand to his cap in a rigid salute.

Americans. Well, well.

'Male? Female?'

'Yep.'

Jack gave Grace a look of what he hoped to be genuine warmth.

'What is it?' she asked uneasily and took a step backward.

'Grace, let me buy you a Tequila Sunrise to go with your beer.'

'What do you want me to do,' she asked, 'lay an egg?'

Jack waited until she had her eyes firmly fixed on the syrupy red grenadine dribbling gently into the tall glass.

'No,' he said in a measured tone of voice, 'I want you to help me make up a foursome.'

Do you love me, Surfer Girl? Her crystalline beauty was wholly American in its androgynous innocence. Goofy front teeth kept the wide, full lips slightly apart giving her face an earnest, inquisitive appearance. Below her pretty, upturned nose, soft, downy, blond hair formed a subtle, sexy moustache. A deep tan almost matched the orangey brown freckles liberally dotted about her face and arms.

'Hi I'm Jack, this is Grace. Hope you don't mind if we join you.'

A loud chorus of 'Well hi there' rang out from the small group

35

of clean-cut teenagers. A swotty, Clark Kent look-alike immediately pounced on Grace and demanded to know all about the difficulties of belonging to an ethnic minority group in a country where the colonialist attitudes were still so prevalent. But Jack's eyes were being held by the Surfer Girl's piercing, blue gaze boring into his soul. Her face read like an open book, she had no idea what or who he was but she sure wanted to find out. Sitting down in the chair next to her, Jack leaned over and put his lips close to her ear.

'My name's Jack Shaw,' he whispered breathily,' I live in a luxurious apartment just around the corner from Buckingham Palace. Impressed?'

The Surfer Girl didn't respond.

'I often sleep with girls without making love to them, can you believe that?'

The Surfer Girl's eyes darted from side to side as though everyone else could hear him as well. 'Hi.' A powerful, resonant voice took Jack by surprise. 'I'm Kathy Springfield and I think you're lying through your teeth.'

An hour later the place was packed. Jack's balls began to ache as Kathy shifted about in his lap. He took a final toke of the joint and passed it to her.

'Is this hash?'

'Sssh, not so loud.'

'What's the matter?' she mouthed silently.

'The guy playing pool right in front of us,' he hissed. The man was about twenty-five with mousy hair cut to medium length and parted on one side. He wore a pair of faded blue denims, an anorak of roughly the same shade and shiny black boots. It was the boots that gave him away. 'Plain clothes.'

'Cops?' Kathy's eyes bulged.

'No sweat, just keep cool.'

'Are you out of your mind?' she seethed. 'We could be busted right here. I'm a goddamn minor, you know?'

'You said you were eighteen and –'

'I'm not old enough to be drinking in a bar, at least, not back home.'

The plain clothes racked up another triangle of pool balls, flipped a coin onto the green baize, won the toss and nominated his opponent to break.

'He's a regular,' Jack explained, 'Sean Binkybonk.'

'Oh come on.' Kathy chuckled despite herself.

'No, I mean I don't know his last name. But he's okay, see, most of the gear we get comes from the big busts. They put Sean in to get acquainted with the dealers then, when they're sure something big's going down, they bust the place. A month later, the same dealers are selling the same gear and Sean's on overtime. It's cat and mouse.'

The wild, fixed grin on Kathy's face relaxed slightly and she blinked rapidly.

'Are you okay? I thought you'd be used to it, you know, Kojak and all that.'

'It's not real life, Jack, believe me.' Kathy inhaled sharply and tossed her shoulder length, dark blond hair from side to side. 'Life in Pittsburgh was pretty dull before I came on this school trip.'

Three weeks of trotting around Europe with your mates didn't sound like any school trip Jack had ever been on. Unless you counted the day trip to Boulogne.

'You're sixteen, Jack, sixteen!' She held out both her hands as though they were supporting an extremely heavy object. 'And you're running around with the key to the goddamn city.'

He loved the way she said that word 'goddamn'.

'Those trousers.' She poked at his brand new, first-time worn, fluorescent yellow jeans. If you stared at the material for long enough, it made you feel dizzy. 'I'd love to be able to wear those at home.'

These were, by far, the most plain and subtle trousers Jack owned. 'What's to stop you?'

She rattled the ice in an otherwise empty glass and smiled firmly. 'Could I get another one of these?'

A haze of green smoke hung in the air and the jukebox pumped out a bass line that shook the floor. Jack walked over to the crowded bar and had to wait several minutes for a space to become available. Slipping in between a couple of debby-looking nubiles, he waved a ten pound note in the air.

'You're really hittin' on this one hard, Jack. You gonna slide into home plate tonight or you gonna hang around third base for a while?' Nick chuckled as he poured a pint for somebody else. 'Yeah, Reggie Jackson ain't got nothin' on you.' He slammed the pint down on the bar. 'That'll be ahhh . . . fifty-two and ahh . . . one thirty – no, wait a minute – one twenty-eight for the screwdr-, aw hell, that can't be right. Now let's see, fifty-two for the screw-, shit, the *beer*. And ah . . . one thirty-eight, yah, one thirty-eight for the 'driver. Altogether that'll be ah . . .'

The doe-eyed deb regarded her drink disconsolately. Froth gushed over the brim of the glass and by the time the beer had settled there was only about an eighth of a pint left. And Nick was overcharging her for the 'driver. Jack was sorely tempted to exploit this classic potential pick-up situation. Instead he ran the scene in his head like an imaginary film:

'Excuse me, but I couldn't help noticing how poorly you two were treated back there at the bar. Shall I have a word with the barman? I'm sure we could get you some better service than that.'

'No thank you, we're managing quite nicely, actually.'

Those sort were always snotty to begin with.

'All right, I'll tell you what. How's about if I get the next round? Lager and a screwdriver is it?'

At this point the 'driver hiccoughs merrily but the lager is adamant.

'We'll buy our own drinks, thank you very much.'

Now for a few probing jabs with the right. 'Uh huh. My money not good enough for ya then?'

The 'driver's staccato hiccoughs become a constant stream of giggles.

A quick flurry of combination punches to the body. 'Let me ask you this. If I offered you a million quid you'd take it, right? If I offered you a thousand or even a hundred, you'd take it.' Momentarily the guard is dropped and there's an opening for a left hook. 'But I'm not trying to pay you to fall in love with me, all I ask is that you let me buy you both a drink. What is that, torture?'

The lager smirks in spite of herself and POW! Two minutes into the first round, the World's Heavyweight Champeen does it again.

'On one condition,' says the lager. 'We get the round after that.'

Music to my ears, dear lady, music to my ears.

Opposite the bar, one of the mohicans gathered around the juke caught Jack's eye and offered a weaselly grin. A grey flannel nappy hung from his backside and the three cotton straps on the inside of each trouser leg were tied to their opposite number.

All at once, a hand thumped down hard onto Jack's shoulder. 'All right?' Pat the Murderer was a cuddly, bullet-shaped man who just happened to have killed somebody once. One night he'd given Jack the juicy details of how an ordinary pub brawl had suddenly turned into a court case. The beer bottle he'd intended to smash over the victim's head didn't break and the blow was fatal. Incredibly, he received a five year sentence, suspended for three. With only a few months to go it looked as though he was going to walk away from it completely.

'How's it going, Pat?' The question, like his, was more of a greeting really and Pat wandered over to the mohicans.

The weasel immediately dipped into his pocket and held out a quid with a shaking hand. Pat accepted the note and waited. Reluctantly, the weasel sidled up to the bar, ordered a pint of lager and blackcurrant and took it back to Pat. If the weasel was smart he would untie his legs and run as fast as they could carry him because Pat hated sycophants. He demanded them but despised them and this weasel character was rushing head on towards the fattest lip of his life. Walking over to the pinball machine Pat hooked his chunky hands underneath the front end and lifted it two feet off the ground. Satisfied the machine was high enough, he whisked his hands away and it crashed to the floor, spitting out ten pence pieces from the reject coin slot. Pat leaned casually against the machine whilst Weasel crawled around the floor picking up the coins that had rolled away in various directions.

Removing his baseball cap, Nick wiped the sweat from his forehead. It wasn't at all hot and Jack felt sorry for the barman who could do nothing but stand by and watch, perhaps making a mental note to tell the manager downstairs that Pat's name must, once more, be added to the list of those not welcome. The bans usually lasted about two weeks, depending on the person and the offence. Fighting, drug-dealing and even prostitution escaped the net but damage to brewery property was something the management simply would not tolerate.

'Fares please.'

Leaning across Kathy, Jack held out two ten pence coins.

'You must be joking,' the leathery faced conductor sneered.

'You wanna see my birth certificate?' From his back pocket, Jack produced a grubby envelope.

The conductor shook his head. 'Could belong to anybody. Look, son, neither of you are under fifteen –'

Kathy snorted drunkenly.

'– so tell me where you wanna go or get off the bus.'

'Okay, okay. Two to Eaton Place.'

'*The* Eaton Place?' asked Kathy.

'Yeah. It's a nice walk from there to my place. Quiet. Why, do you know it?'

'*The* Eaton Place,' Kathy repeated. 'Like in *Upstairs, Downstairs* on the TV?'

Jack giggled helplessly. 'I thought you had to be somebody's grandmother to enjoy that show.'

Kathy burst into tears. 'Oh Jack, I've never known anyone else like you. What are we gonna do?'

In twenty-four hours she would be three thousand miles away. 'Haven't you got a boyfriend?'

She shook her head and sobbed.

Though he was two years her junior, Jack felt an almost paternal love for her.

Four

Blinking in the sunlight, Andy pulled his Fred Perry shirt over his head. Underneath the bed he found a pair of twenty-one hole Dr Marten boots and laced them swiftly. Looking in the mirror, he saw his cream-coloured Levi stay-press trousers were marked with a faded orange stain and he cursed. Another pair of stay-press hung over the back of the chair, with braces already attached and he began untying the boots. Examining his hair in the bathroom mirror, he fingered the two pencil-thin lines, shaved about an inch apart, that began at his left temple and ran along the side of his head down to his neck. The rest of his head was covered in hair no longer than the old man's stubble. The Polish barber at Fulham Broadway gave the best number one cut in town and Andy visited him every other Tuesday come rain or shine. Other skins would leave their hair growing for weeks until they were in danger of becoming fuckin' 'ippies but Andy knew better than that. To be a true skin, your hair had to be right and, if it wasn't, all the tattoos and criminal convictions in the world wouldn't make up for it.

'NF WOGS OUT'. Andy stepped back from the lift wall to admire his handiwork. He breathed in the tangy fumes of spray paint, his favourite smell. The slogan looked good in blood red but it needed something extra, something really fuckin' 'eavy. 'OR ELSE . . .' Yeah, that was perfect. All the Winstons and Errolls and Juniors would shit their pants and go back to where they came from, or so he hoped. Maybe then the old man might be able to get a decent job again instead of pissing away his dole money every day. Things had been all right until he lost his job on the buses but they'd been going steadily downhill ever since. And who do you think took his place? Happy Mr Sambo, that's who. Nobody really believed all that bollocks about some bird claiming she'd been molested by him, it was the nig-nogs taking over. Them and the Pakis.

The change in the bus conductor's pouch jingled as he bounded up the stairs. Letting his head droop lazily to one side, Andy closed his eyes and pretended to be asleep. 'Eeny more?' Standing just a few inches away from him, the conductor rattled his pouch deliberately. Andy's head jiggled and bounced lightly on the window as the bus turned into Victoria Street. The conductor waited for several moments and then wandered back down the aisle. Bunking the fare like this was a doddle.

Andy jumped out at the stop before Jack's and went into the off license. Special Brew was sixty-five pence a can up here, daylight bloody robbery. He wondered how Robert Hardcastle was getting on. The Hardcastles were, by name and nature, the toughest organisation in the area. An extended family of villains. Robert was the youngest, an asthmatic shrimp who was fuckin' lucky he had brothers. And cousins. Lots of people would have had his guts for garters otherwise, Andy included. But coming across the Hardcastles at school had been a real education. There was that time when Robert and his elder brother Paul had some trouble with the blacks in the fifth year. Some wog threatened that half of Brixton was gonna come down the school and beat shit out of them. At three thirty the next day there were five massive black geezers waiting at the school gate. Each one had a kitbag. At three thirty-five they were lined up against the wall, spread-eagled, being searched by the Old Bill. The kitbags contained axes and one of the geezers had an air-pistol shoved down his bollocks. At three forty-five they were on the receiving end of a tasty licking, courtesy of Police Constable Peter Hardcastle and his trusty colleagues. No charges were brought against the wogs. They got off light. Andy's stride loosened up as the beer went to work and he bobbed along the pavement. It was funny how one Brew made all the difference.

'SACHA. BACK AT 4. LOVE G.' He studied the note pinned to the door once more. This gift horse had the words Andrew Mason branded into its flank. He looked at his watch. Three forty-four. Perfect. Sliding the corridor window open, Andy hitched himself onto the sill. The four-floor drop down to the basement was sheer and deadly. But Jack's kitchen window was next to the corridor window and could be reached easily if the iron drainpipes separating them were secure. Swinging across, Andy glanced down and was treated to a breathtaking perspective but, as he landed on the concrete sill, it slipped away beneath him. Clinging on to the solid black pipes, he kicked and scrambled back to his original position. The nearest half of the kitchen sill was covered in slimy, brown grease. It looked like pre-historic chip fat and probably was. He swung again. Crouching on the dry half, he slid the window open, eased himself through legs first and landed in a bowl full of dirty dishes. In water. It had been raining earlier on so, if anybody asked, he'd fallen down and sat in a puddle.

Jack hadn't shown him around the flat the first time he'd visited, so Andy decided to work through the rooms systematically. Opposite the kitchen was a blank, white door. He opened it and guessed immediately that this was the bird's room. A large poster of Richard Keyes dominated one wall and smaller photographs of the same subject surrounded a large dressing-table mirror. Andy looked more closely and saw that, in one of the pictures, Keyes was kissing a coloured bird. She was nice. But somehow the photo didn't look right. He ran his finger lightly across the surface. He could just feel the subtle join. So this was Grace. She must like the bloke an awful lot to go to all this trouble. The top drawer of the dressing table was full of socks and pants and . . . aye aye . . . what's this? A brown leather purse. Could it possibly be that . . . ahh, shame. Andy held up the large, pink, plastic device and regarded it disappointedly. Evidently she fucked like a nigger or she wouldn't have dildos lying about all over the place but that information wasn't gonna do him any good. Firstly, she had a boyfriend and secondly, he wouldn't be caught dead shaggin' a coon. Even if she was nice looking.

As he made his way along the hall to the next room, a key slid into the front door lock. Striding calmly but quickly back to the kitchen, Andy heaved himself onto the draining board. Crawling out onto the dry half of the sill, he waited until he heard the front door slam shut and then swung back across the drainpipe and in through the corridor window. He paused for a moment before ringing the bell.

'Yes?' Grace regarded him unflinchingly. Her ebony skin shone like a panther's coat. Though she was quite a lot shorter than he, she still seemed very tall. She wore a huge, floppy, pink jumper and long, multi-coloured leg warmers over a pair of purple tights. She was firm. 'Who was it you wanted?' she asked patiently.

'Do I get a choice?' Andy replied and she smiled a brilliant white. 'I like your smile.' It got wider, if that was possible.

'Do I know you?' She frowned as though she might have met him somewhere before and forgotten.

'Do you want to?' Sometimes the verbals came out just right. Especially after a Brew.

'No seriously,' she giggled, 'who did you want to see?'

Andy gazed around the corridor casually. 'Well, like I said, if you could tell me 'oo's at 'ome, I'll be able to make a firm decision on that.'

'We could play this game all day. Except that I haven't the time.'

He was losing her. Plan B. 'Andrew Mason – born nine five sixty-one – weight nine and a half stone – colour of eyes blue – education St Matthew's Primary, Westminster Comprehensive –occupation government artist – favourite hob –'

'Government artist? What's that supposed to mean?'

'I draw the dole.' She beamed again. Bingo. 'Jack about? We're old mates. Went to the same school in Pimlico.'

'Westminster.' She nodded.

'Affirmative, Captain. I thought I'd pop in on the off chance. But if he's out . . .'

'. . . I s'pose I ought to be shootin' off,' said Andy, hoping that Grace would persuade him otherwise. After giving her the full SP on his criminal activities to date, he had listened as she told him about herself. She was twenty-two and beginning to worry about it. During the last eighteen months she'd been modelling for the hairdressing salon where Sacha, her brother, worked as a cutter. But, although that meant free hair and beauty treatment, she didn't get paid and the work wasn't really leading anywhere. Sure, she wanted to be a full-time model but it was an over-crowded, cut-throat business and unless you had (a) good contacts or (b) a lucky break, it was well nigh impossible to get started. Plus, she was about two inches too short, measuring five feet four and three-quarters. She first met Jack at the salon when Sacha's boss was trying out his latest invention. Just the idea that somebody would be prepared to walk around sporting leopard skin hair had prompted her to strike up a conversation. If you knew Jack at all, then you also knew it was impossible for him to remain at close quarters with a girl for more than five minutes without trying to make her. Unfortunately for Jack, that privilege had gone to Otto. Now she was drifting aimlessly without a proper job or boyfriend. She felt she really ought to be doing something, if only she could figure out what. At school, her music teacher had said she had a fine voice but, what with the advent of punk, melodic singing was suddenly very unhip. She produced a Diana Ross LP and sang along to 'Touch Me In The Morning'. Back in the Sixties, Motown had groomed their artists for stardom, like the Rank School of Charm, until they could dance and act, as well as sing. The possibilities were endless once you had that basic training. But where were the opportunities for a new Diana Ross now? Still, things weren't all that bad. Her family were very supportive so she had the financial freedom to go out most nights and have a good time.

'Where are you off to?' she asked politely.

'Nowhere really,' he shrugged.

'Well, Sacha should be coming over any time now. There's an exhibition at the Tate Gallery that he desperately wants to see.' She wrinkled her nose. 'Sir Archibald somebody or other, it all sounds deathly boring to me but you're welcome to come along.'

'Great.' He wasn't kidding either. Bunking off from school, he and Jack had occasionally popped into the Tate. Jack couldn't stand it and moaned constantly about the stuffiness, the lack of seats and the overall, mind-numbing boredom. But Andy had been astonished by the variety of colour and form. Except for that Pollock geezer. Now there was a bloke who'd managed to pull the wool over everybody's eyes, like the tailors who 'made' the emperor's new clothes. Andy remembered the mass of black, squiggly lines with amusement. You had to admire the geezer's neck.

Half an hour later, Sacha still hadn't shown up. 'It's just like him,' Grace sighed, 'I always add an hour whenever he tells me what time he's coming. It can be bloody annoying sometimes.'

'Yeah, I know what you mean. My mate Carl's a bit like that.'

The Churchill skins were a force to be reckoned with in West London. Carl was the leader and, at the age of eighteen, the eldest. In a year or two they could start putting their strength to more practical use. Football was for kids, what Carl had in mind was the big league, extortion and protection. Most Paki proprietors would be more than willing to part with a fiver for a shop window or a daughter's cherry remaining intact.

'If 'e doesn't show up maybe we could –'

The phone rang. Grace stared at him for several seconds before getting up to answer it.

'Sacha? Oh good, I was . . . Oh, why? Not again? It's a wonder he doesn't ask you to tie his bloody shoelaces . . . No. No, really. Just sitting about.' Glancing over to Andy, she gave him a sly, sexy smile. 'That's okay. Yeah. Next time perhaps you'll tell him to go and play with the traffic . . . Yeah . . . Ha ha. Take care, byyyeeeee!' Turning to Andy, she arched her back provocatively. 'You were saying?'

'I was gonna suggest we go alone,' he shrugged, 'but then I remembered that you didn't really wanna go anyway.'

'No,' she agreed, 'not really.'

''Ow about a bite to eat?' That was a fuckin' stupid thing to say when he had the sum total of one pound and forty seven pence in his pocket.

Trees reached out of the ground like sinister, skeletal hands. Wind whipped silently through the barren branches and Andy wondered why he didn't feel cold. Grass grew in small clumps amongst the mud, making the whole park look like a giant pile of horseshit. He got all his best ideas here. Winter was bare and sparse, leaving room to think and breathe. Not like summer, when the park was full of fuckin' kids and the stench of flowers made you wanna throw up. And insects crawled on your arms and up your nose, spreading their filthy disease. And the women walked around with their fat arses hanging out of their shorts and peeling red cleavages giving way to sagging, blue veined breasts. Andy was never a tit man. Didn't see why people made such a fuss about them. They were just sacks of skin filled with gristle and fat like a dodgy meat-pie.

'Excuse me, do you know what time it is?'

The bird had tight jeans digging into her fanny. In his sitting position on the park bench, Andy found his mouth level with her crotch. Shame about the kid. As the woman wiggled away with her son, Andy wondered whether giving birth had loosened her up. When he shagged his first bird he wanted her to scream in agony when she felt it going in.

As he lay in bed that night, Andy masturbated and thought of Grace. She leaned forward over a pool table, a pair of jeans around her ankles and he stood behind, gripping her firm ass with both hands. She responded by slamming back into him. He grunted and quickened the pace until he could go no faster, their wet skin slapped together and the heavy, slate table shifted slightly. Reaching out, he grabbed a handful of her beaded plaits and pulled them roughly from side to side like horses' reins and she tightened around him.

Five

Tuesday

Dear Kathy,

   Re our last telephone conversation. The mountain is coming to Mohammed. In other words, cancel all planned activities from December 22nd for ten days. I'll fly into New York and catch a train from there to Pittsburgh. Don't worry about accommodation, I can always check into a cheap hotel. I know it sounds crazy, what with Christmas and all, but we're auditioning for a new vocalist and it's the only time I can get away. Let me know if there's a problem.

I love you,

Jack

PS I'll ring you from the station.

Jack's stomach knotted and he started to grind his teeth slowly. The seats were crammed too close together and he had lost the feeling in his right leg.

   'Ladies and gentlemen, would you please fasten your seat belts and extinguish all cigarettes. It is now seven forty-three p.m. New York time and we will be landing in approximately ten minutes.'

   And not a moment too soon either. Jack's first ever flight had turned out to be the most boring experience of his entire life. He'd made the mistake of not renting a headset, thinking that the movie would still be pretty good without sound. Endless, static shots of Richard Dreyfuss and Marsha Mason jabbering on had proved otherwise. The constant wave of laughter rippling up and down the fuselage, as the three separate screens delivered their punch-lines at different times, simply rubbed salt into the wound. There was nothing to do but observe the other passengers and try to imagine how each of them would react should the plane crash. At least if the movie had been *Airport* the bastards wouldn't be laughing.

'Jesus!' Jack was totally unnerved. A huge wooden butt hung menacingly from the holster of every airport security guard in sight. He hurried to collect his luggage, anxious to be somewhere else. Having retrieved his bag he made his way to the customs area.

'Open the bag, please.'

Jack did as he was told. The customs official began sorting her way through the various layers of underwear, T-shirts and trousers.

'Uh huh.' She waved the copy of *Junky* by William Burroughs in front of Jack's face, conveniently cooling the beads of sweat about to form on his forehead. She probably thought it was some kind of crazy double bluff. After all, who'd be stupid enough to smuggle drugs into the country whilst carrying a book with a title like that? 'Would you mind stepping this way, sir?' Did he have a choice?

Behind the customs counter, a door marked 'Private' opened into an ominously sparse, white room. Jack smiled casually as the official ran her eyes up and down his body, licking her top lip.

'Undress,' she barked.

It was impossible to tell what was going on behind her mirrored shades and Jack's crotch bulged with an anticipatory hard-on. He concentrated his mind on an image of Grace and his hard-on diminished as he stood, cold and shivering in his underpants.

'Undress,' the official repeated calmly, 'and turn around.'

The sound of rustling polythene sent the blood rushing to his crotch once more and he felt a smooth, dry hand brush lightly against his shoulder blades. Being very ticklish, he leaned forward instinctively. 'Unnnhhh.' Two long fingers squished, unpleasantly, into his anus.

Jack found the main exit and jumped into a yellow cab. 'Penn Station.'

'You got it.'

On the glass partition in front of him, the name Sandy Fernandez underlined a photograph of a psychotic-looking Mexican. Señor Loco.

'Hey bro', you Eenglish, right? I got a niece in Leeverpool. Rosa, Rosa Fernandez, you know her?'

Señor Loco didn't look like the kind of guy who'd take no for an answer. A hundred yards further down the freeway, the lights changed from green to red and the cab screeched into top gear, hurtling suicidally toward the busy intersection.

'She's real pretty, about your age. What are you, nineteen, twenty?' Señor Loco hollered as the engine screamed in overworked agony.

Gripping the plastic upholstery, Jack watched in mute terror as cars slowly began to pull into the junction. Nineteen? Twenty? He wasn't even going to live that long. Oh please, please, God, give us wings. Now.

'Fuckayoseesteranyomamayacocksuckingsonovabeetch,' Señor Loco bawled and abandoned the steering wheel in order to physically emphasise his disgust as the cab sailed between the two honking cars, missing them by inches. 'Am I right?'

Right? To be playing chicken in a two-ton hunk of tin at eighty-five miles an hour? Right!?

'Yeah, she wrote me what was happening over there, punk rock, kids dressing up like Hallowe'en and shit. She's into it, man. You sure you never met her?'

Jack prayed silently for Rosa, wherever she was, to please come and take her uncle's place at the wheel.

'London,' he gasped, 'I'm from London. I – I don't – I've only been to Liverpool once.' Emerging from the windowless back of the tour van, he had performed on stage at Eric's, climbed back into the van and returned to London.

'I tell you bro', once you meet Rosa, you don' forget. She's wild, man.' Again his hands left the wheel, this time to draw an imaginary hour glass figure. Short bursts of high-pitched wheezing rattled in Señor Loco's chest and his shoulders jiggled up and down in merriment. 'Whoo! Rosa, hah cha chaaa. Err . . . one four four . . .' He scratched a patch of greasy hair above his ear. 'One four four err . . . High Street. Yeah, tha's where she leeve. You ever go there?'

At last the cab pulled up in front of Penn Station and Jack rummaged around the bag for his wallet. It was three days before Christmas and he intended to give a generous tip. The wallet was gone.

Señor Loco waited for Jack to cash a traveller's cheque in a nearby liquor store and thanked him for the generous tip.

The last train to Pittsburgh had left an hour ago and the obese ticket officer was doing her best not to help. Jack asked to be directed to the nearest coach station and she spat out the words so savagely he decided not to repeat the question even though he hadn't understood the answer.

The liquor store owner was much more helpful and Jack soon found himself at the Bestway bus terminal. Hundreds of people milled around excitedly as he pushed his way to the ticket office. A bus to Indianapolis was due to leave in forty minutes with Pittsburgh on its list of stop-off points. The return ticket price left him with the princely sum of sixty-three dollars to spend during his ten-day visit. He hoped Kathy's folks would be full of the Christmas spirit.

The bus was alive with chattering voices and smiling faces. Sitting next to Jack was a boy of similar age, watching him intently.

'Say, are you from England?'

He'd never imagined his nationality could be so conspicuous. 'Yes.'

'Well hi, I'm Butch, where you headed?' They shook hands.

'My name's Jack, pleased to meet you. Actually I'm on my way to Pittsburgh.'

Butch nodded and waited expectantly for him to elaborate.

'Er . . . there's a girl I met in London and we . . . I mean –'

'I got you buddy. I'm going back home to Indianapolis for Christmas, get me some a that home cookin', you know?'

They small-talked for a while then Butch leaned over and said in a low voice, 'You wanna smoke?' He held out two small joints and jerked a thumb towards the back of the bus. 'Do it in the toilet.'

Leaning out of the window Jack blew smoke into the darkness. The sky looked strangely different as the sound of carol singing drifted down from the front of the bus. He opened the toilet door to find Butch and a dozen or so others tearing into a gospel version of 'Good King Wenceslas'.

'Cut the crap or we stop right here,' the driver boomed over the loud speakers. 'I'm only gonna warn you people once.'

A solitary voice took up the tune of 'Swing low, sweet chariot' and the bus screamed to a halt. Without a word the driver jumped out. Several minutes passed and then at last he returned triumphantly.

'I think we understand each other,' the speakers crackled.

There was no more singing.

Jack glanced at Butch's watch. It was three o'clock in the morning and they'd been on the road for six hours.

'I ain't never been to England,' Butch mumbled thickly. 'I wanna see the queen.' He came from a poor family who felt lucky their son had a job even if it was only washing dishes. He preferred to live in New York because it had a 'pulse'. 'They live in slow motion everywhere else,' he explained. 'In the Apple there are places to go, people to meet. Like you, you know?'

Jack wanted to know what Butch thought of Pittsburgh.

'Oh man! Steeltown USA. We call it "the pits",' he chuckled throatily. 'No, I'm just kidding. My cousin lives there, got a good job too.'

Kathy's father was a doctor and in America that meant she could have her own car. Jack pictured the two of them in the back seat of an old Studebaker. Maybe there would be a jealous boyfriend he could dispatch in a thrilling fist fight. 'Have you got a girl?'

Butch snored.

Something sharp dug into Jack's rib cage. 'Hey Jack, we're here.'

A brightly lit waiting room ran the length of a terminal that was otherwise deserted.

'Have a good time,' Butch shouted as Jack stepped off the bus. 'Maybe I'll see you in England.'

At one end of the waiting room stood a row of six chairs. Mounted on the left arm of each chair was a tiny television. Jack sat in the nearest chair and swivelled the TV round to face him. In the top right hand corner a coin slot had 25c written beneath it. He fed the machine and was treated to three minutes of cartoons sandwiched between seven minutes of commercials. An hour later he could stand the tedium no longer and hoped that six a.m. wasn't too early to be announcing his arrival.

'Unnhh.' The voice was male and groggy with exhaustion.

Jack hung up. There was no point in getting off on the wrong foot with her father and waiting another couple of hours wouldn't hurt. He walked over to a soft-drinks dispenser and selected an unfamiliar brand name. It tasted like liquid polystyrene.

At seven forty-five he tried again.

'Yes?' The voice was now chipper and relaxed.

'Mr Springfield, I'm Jack Shaw, a friend of Kathy's.'

'I'm afraid Kathy is asleep at the moment, could you call back?'

'Yes I suppose – well, actually, would it be possible to wake her? It is rather urgent.'

There was a brief pause. 'Was it you who called earlier?'

'Me? No, sir.'

Jack had already put in two more quarters when Kathy finally picked up the receiver.

'Hello.'

'Kathy, it's me, Jack.'

'Jack? Where are you?'

'I'm at the Bestway bus station, can you meet me here?'

The Volkswagen sped away from the terminal.

'Did you get my letter?' Kathy pressed a button on the dashboard and her window slid open.

'Which one?' Jack did the same and grinned as his own window opened automatically.

'The one I sent two weeks ago.'

'No, not yet. Why, was it important?'

Kathy turned to look at him. 'Oh, Jack, you shouldn't have come.'

'Why not?' She sounded like a schoolteacher telling a pupil he'd been a bad boy.

'Mom and Dad are very strict. I told you we better wait until . . .' She trailed off.

The house was enormous and as they bounced up the steep driveway Jack was reminded of the credit sequence from a TV situation comedy. The narrator would introduce the characters and then the opening dialogue always took place in the family living room.

'Do you have relatives here?' Springfield was an imposing man, well over six feet tall with a bushy red beard.

'I have an uncle in Philadelphia.' They had never met and were unlikely to do so. 'I thought I'd hang around here for a few days and see the sights.'

Springfield eyed him quizzically. 'You won't find much to do in Pittsburgh at Christmas time. Kathy's going to be pretty busy helping her Mom with the decorations. Maybe you should go to Philly and have yourself a family Christmas.'

'Oh I think it'd be a shame to leave after I only just got here, don't you?'

Gravel crunched under the tyres as the Volkswagen nosed into the motel car park.

'I didn't do too well did I?' Jack was aware that, if there had been a chance of him staying with her family, then he'd blown it.

'How much money do you have?'

'Sixty-three dollars. I lost the rest somewhere over the Atlantic.'

Reaching into the purse on her lap, Kathy produced a handful of notes.

'No – look I can't take your money. It – it's not right.'

'But –'

'No.'

The beady-eyed desk clerk stared hard at Kathy. 'Don't I know you?'

'My friend is just helping me settle in, she won't be staying.'

'Okay, here y'are.' Jack took the key. 'It's number six at the far end and, remember, no visitors after ten o'clock.'

The motel consisted of seven pre-fab boxes laid end to end. Inside Jack's box was a single bed, a black and white TV and a shower.

'It's not much, is it?' Kathy said softly.

No it wasn't but at least here they could be alone. 'When will you be able to get away?'

'After dinner tonight. I'll tell Dad I'm at Angie's, she'll cover for me.'

Jack was ravenous. A Burger King was open just down the road so he showered and put on a clean T-shirt.

'One whopper, two packs of french fries and a large coke, please.'

Gaudy yellows and bright greens conjured up a circus atmosphere with the staff as clowns in their striped aprons and cardboard hats.

'Anything else?'

Judging from her size, the woman behind the counter obviously viewed his order as a small snack.

Back in the motel room Jack dozed in front of a football game.

Mr Dodds, the desk clerk, was busily counting money in reception when Kathy tip-toed across the dark car park.

'I took a real chance coming here,' she whispered as Jack closed the door.

'It's all right, I've already checked the room for bugs,' he laughed.

'I'm serious, Jack, I could get into a lot of trouble.' She sat down on the bed and folded her arms. 'That's really what I've come to talk to you about. You see it's Dad . . .'

As he listened Jack grew more and more incredulous until finally he could contain himself no longer.

'You mean this is it?' he exploded, interrupting Kathy's flow.

Her lower lip trembled.

'This is it?' Jack repeated. 'No more?' Thick veins stood out on his muscular arms as he clenched his fists. 'I don't believe it.'

Pacing around the floor in tiny circles, he clutched at his forehead. 'Jesus Christ, woman, you're eighteen years old.'

A fluorescent yellow speck was still visible in the rear-view mirror as Kathy waited impatiently for a green light.

Half a mile down the road Jack sat on his bag next to the bus stop. An old man limped towards him. He eyed Jack disdainfully and spat on the sidewalk. Jack hoped his uncle would be full of the Christmas spirit.

Six

Once or twice a month Chrissy would stop off at Jack's flat on her way to or from work. It was good to see one of the family get involved in the music business. The Destroyers were a third rate punk band but Jack's drumming talent would soon bring him better offers. She might even be able to lend him a hand if he let her. She admired Nat for allowing her son to leave home at such an early age. 'What else could I do? Tie him to a chair?' Walking through the private courtyard, she wished Phyllis had been as open minded.

Lions and griffins scowled down at her from the huge stone fountain that occupied the courtyard centre. Plush carpet and flock wallpaper inside the lift had always reminded her of a minute Indian restaurant. Chrissy jabbed at the doorbell and bit her lower lip.

'All right?'

Him! Looking even more evil and unpleasant than ever. That hair – he had no blessed hair – he was a bald stick insect, an awkward, evil ugliness.

Andy swayed slightly and put one hand against the wall to steady himself. 'You comin' in, are ya?'

Andrew Mason, she knew a thing or two about him all right. Nat and Ben had been far too lax about their son's association with this particular boy. And now he was back, how long would it be before Mason's presence brought this flat to the attention of the police?

Grace lay sprawled across two beanbags in front of a large

colour television. Mason flopped down beside her and slid his hand into her crotch. That would end in tears and no mistake.

'Grace,' Chrissy barked angrily, 'where's Jack? Is he at the Roebuck?' She had always refused to set foot in that filthy place.

'No. Didn't he tell you?'

'Didn't tell no one by the sound of it,' Mason chortled. 'World's biggest bleedin' secret.'

'He's gone to America,' Grace continued casually.

'Jesus my – When? Why?'

'A whirlwind romance with a girl from Pittsburgh, Pennsylvania,' Grace enunciated each syllable with great care.

She was drunk, silly bitch.

'You've missed him by about . . .' Grabbing Andy's wrist, Grace tried to focus her eyes on the digits. '. . . a day,' she announced brightly and collapsed with laughter.

Jack could be pretty irresponsible at times but he wasn't a complete fool. Mason was at the bottom of this. Without asking for permission, Chrissy marched over to the telephone and snatched the receiver from its cradle.

'Hello, Nat?'

'Chris, how nice. I was j–'

'Nat, where's Jack? Do you know? Do you know what's going on?'

'Oh, I'm sorry Chris, didn't he tell you? Typical. He's gone to Pittsburgh. To see a girl, if you can believe that,' she laughed.

But it was no laughing matter. To get to Pennsylvania you had to land in New York.

'I hope he'll be all right. I am trying not to worry but it's very difficult. You've been over there Chris, what's it like?'

'Big.'

'I know, I know,' Nat sighed in wonderment.

'I could tell you about where I've been but . . .'

'I hope he'll be all right. Do you think he'll be safe?'

For all her fear and loathing of America, Chrissy couldn't really see anything getting the better of Jack. He was so . . . ignorant. Blissfully unaware. 'Yes,' she said, 'Yes I do.'

After accepting an invitation to dinner on Christmas Day, she hung up. Mason and Grace had their tongues down each other's throats. A scrambling, screaming guitar solo became audible. She would say hello and goodbye to Otto before leaving.

The ferocious feedback stopped abruptly as Chrissy knocked gently on his bedroom door. Looking drawn and tired, Otto frowned in concentration.

'Chrissy?' He stared right through her as though she were invisible.

'Yes.'

'Oh.' Otto moved his head from side to side whilst his eyes remained locked in one position, like a blind man. 'I, uh . . .'

'Are you okay?'

'Yeah, sure. Come in, have a seat.'

There were no chairs so she sat, straight backed and formal, on the edge of his bed. Perhaps Prissy would have been a more suitable name for Phyllis's youngest.

'Would you like a . . .' Otto waved a thin smoking cylinder decorated with the star-spangled banner.

'It looks like a firework,' she laughed. And so harmless.

'Yeah, I had a arabation and bought these.' Otto pulled out a drawer full of cigarette papers, each packet with a different design.

He sounded more Swedish than usual. Maybe he was nervous. Chrissy laughed again.

'Mmm,' she grunted, accepting the joint. The sensation was clean and pure, quite unlike the thick musk of tobacco. 'Do you know anything about this American girl?'

Otto coughed with amusement and fingered the fretboard of his guitar lightly. 'Not really. They spent a lot of time together but ahh . . . she never stayed, you know?'

'Overnight?'

Otto grinned shyly and nodded.

'That's unusual, for Jack.' Her nephew wasn't exactly backward in coming forward. And now he was charging around after the one that got away. 'Was she pretty?'

'Mm,' Otto considered. 'Very American. She's tall and thin, quite uh . . . man-mannish?'

'Masculine,' she corrected him. 'What happened to his T and A obsession, I wonder?'

'Huh?'

'T and A, tits and ass.' Suddenly her cheeks flushed and glowed.

Otto coughed unnecessarily and examined the floor.

'Could we have another of these do you think?' Holding up the star-spangled roach, Chrissy smiled and blinked lazily. Her eyes felt puffy and hunger gnawed at her stomach like a rat. It was as though she'd had a long, hard, physically exhausting day and she felt the euphoria of achievement and satisfaction.

Unstrapping his guitar, Otto leaned over and grabbed a packet of papers. This time they were made to look like hundred dollar bills.

'If it's no trouble.' Chrissy watched as he picked a piece of dried green herb from out of a plastic bag and crumbled it onto the dressing table.

'This is really nice,' Otto drawled. 'We don't usually get a chance to talk.'

Otto's fridge was chock-a-block with goodies and Chrissy's mouth watered. Hurriedly, she grabbed three eggs which she cracked into a bowl and whisked. An unopened family-sized bag of McCain oven chips nestled invitingly in the icebox. Emptying the contents onto a greased baking tray, Chrissy noticed the legend 'serves 6–8' printed on the side. The omelette began to take shape in a frying pan as she peeled apart two rashers of smoked bacon and slipped them under the grill. Immediately the kitchen filled with a pungent aroma and the sound of sizzling fat. If there was one thing she missed about eating meat it was that gorgeous crackle. One large green pepper, one Spanish onion, a handful of button mushrooms and some fresh garlic were diced and scattered into the frying pan. While she waited for the food to cook, Chrissy sliced herself a cheese and tomato sandwich.

'Wow!' Otto marvelled at the feast. 'Is this all for me?'

'Uh huh,' Chrissy grunted, her mouth already full. They sat on the edge of the bed with their plates on their knees.

'No bacon?'

'No I don't eat meat.'

'Oh I hope you didn't mind –'

'No. I'm not one of those obsessive types. I just never really liked the taste and then, when you hear those horrific stories about factory farming and those poor animals being force fed and crippled by – oh,' she sniggered. 'I take it you're not the world's most keen cook? Me neither. I don't mind cooking for myself but I can't understand how anyone could enjoy doing it for more than a couple of people at a time. Who does the shopping? Grace?'

In an effort to retain a mouthful of food, Otto snorted violently and swallowed. 'Fat chance. No, Mum bought it the last time she came over. Apparently I'm losing too much weight.' He grinned.

Though he was rather thin, it suited him.

Without knocking, Grace waltzed into the room, dragging the Mason boy behind her. 'I – oh. I was going to ask you if you wanted anything from Duckmonald's but I can see you are otherwise engaged,' she slurred and they staggered back out again.

Otto frowned.

'You still like her a lot, don't you?'

A pack of Marlboro lay on top of the dressing table and he lit one. His room was very personal and, in that sense, reminded Chrissy of her own. On one side there lay heaps of American comic books. Superman, Batman, the Hulk and quite a few unfamiliar names.

'Who's this Submariner guy? What does he do?'

Otto's eyes came alive as he snapped out of his daze. 'Ah hah.' He held up one finger knowledgeably. 'Namor, Prince of the lost city of Atlantis. On land he has the strength of twenty men while underwater he has no equal. His winged feet enable him to fly –'

'Like that Greek guy, the winged messenger?'

'Hermes, yeah. But,' Otto's voice became grave, 'like all super heroes he has a weakness. Every moment he is out of water, his powers gradually diminish and if he remains on land for too long . . .'

Beer and saliva maintained their separate identities like oil on water in revolting, filmy puddles. It was a very slippery mixture and Chrissy felt glad to be wearing baseball boots. Other female customers in the Roebuck were not so lucky. Like the girl in the stiletto heels sipping her lager through a straw and leaning against the wall to stop herself from toppling over. She had 'victim' written all over her. Black lipstick clashed with the bloodless pale pink of her gums and a chain ran from her nostril to her earlobe like a communications cord on a train. 'Pull this cord only in an emergency.' There certainly would be an emergency if anybody did. The atmosphere was heavy with smoke and sweat and the jukebox was on far too loud.

Otto leaned into Chrissy's face and she recoiled instinctively.

'What do you want to drink?' he shouted.

Instead of catering to a majority of punks, as she had expected, the pub seemed to be full of greasy, middle-aged bikers. The kind who'd rape their grandmother before they sold her.

'Tomato juice,' she hollered, wanting to keep her wits about her.

The victim looked up from her drink and scrutinised Chrissy with snake eyes. Her pendulous breasts were clearly visible beneath a fishnet top and Chrissy's gaze locked onto the light brown area surrounding her nipples. Slowly the victim eased herself away from the wall and tottered towards Chrissy, her breasts jiggling like jelly that had yet to set. When she was mere inches away, the victim looked Chrissy up and down and gave her a sly grin. She took another step forward and Chrissy froze as she felt the coarse strands of nylon brush against her bare arm and the soft flesh of the victim's breast yield under contact.

'Wanna know where I got it?' the victim asked in a harsh caw.

'Excuse me?' Chrissy shuddered as she sensed the victim's, nipple stiffen and push into her arm.

'This top,' the victim explained, 'would you like to know where to get one?'

'Here you go.' Otto hoisted the tomato juice over her shoulder. 'I see you two've met. How's it going, Jaz?' They exchanged pleasantries and then Otto led Chrissy over to a couple of vacant chairs.

'Who was that?'

'Jaz? Oh she's one of Jack's ex'.'

Jesus my beads.

Seven

Grace looked tired and she picked a piece of dried sleep from the corner of her eye. Shit. He'd been in the area since nine thirty, wondering how long he should wait before calling for her. At ten thirty he had begun to drop his bottle, so he took a deep breath and hoped for the best.

'Oh it's you,' she tried to smile but failed.

What a fuck-up. Good job he already had a Brew inside him otherwise he wouldn't have been able to say what he was about to. 'I came back because I 'ad to see ya. I've been up 'alf the night thinkin' about you. I really – I really like ya.' He felt himself blush.

'You're joking, aren't you?' A smile came to her face like a flower opening at incredibly high speed. 'Jack put you up to it, didn't he?'

Andy stood gawping. What could he say? Grace gazed at him quizzically. Pure embarrassment had shrunk his previous hard on.

'He didn't, did he?' Realising the truth, she seemed even more amused.

It wasn't just his prick now, Andy felt small all over. Folding her arms, Grace leaned against the door frame. Something was happening. Andy didn't know whether it was good or bad. Yes he did. It was both.

'Well I'm flattered, I really am. It's a lovely compliment but . . .' She hesitated for a moment. 'What's in the bag?' she asked inquisitively, noticing the white plastic carrier bag he held in his left hand. 'Flowers?' she joked and raised her fine eyebrows humorously.

'Nah. 'S lager. Listen, I'm sorry I woke you up, it was really bad timin'.' No point in playing safe anymore. He tried that yesterday and look where it got him. On a number eleven straight back to poxy Fulham. This time it was all or nothing. 'Here.' Reaching into the carrier bag, he lobbed a can at Grace and she caught it. 'Nothin' like it first fing in the mornin'. Tell Jack to gimme a bell when 'e gets back.'

Grace passed the can from one hand to the other, it had just come out of the fridge and was still very cold. 'I don't think I could drink all this on my own.'

She was a bit of all right was Grace. How many other birds would have treated him to a meal? And she bought all them beers.

'Why's she hanging around the flat?' Andy asked, as they stumbled along Victoria Street towards McDonald's.

At first, Andy hadn't recognised the weird-looking woman at the front door. It wasn't until she started going on about Jack, that he had placed the face. The last time he'd seen Chrissy, she was scowling at him across the austere juvenile court room. Jack's mum was crying her eyes out and his aunty was screwing Andy so badly he'd wanted to walk over and give her a spank in the mouth. Nobody had a right to stare at him in that way. 'Watchew on about?'

'Maybe she fancies Otto.'

'Get away,' Andy laughed, 'she's as bent as a corkscrew.'

'Gay?' Grace's eyes widened incredulously. 'Chrissy? How can you tell?'

'There's a couple a' birds on my block just like 'er. Skinny, flat-chested, don't wear no make-up, you know, all a' that.' Listening with great interest, Grace nodded fervently. 'Yeah, well, they live togevver, don't they?'

'So?'

'So, no one's ever seen a geezer wivvin spittin' distance of their gaff. Now come on, two birds, no blokes, 's well dodgy that is.'

'Hmm,' Grace acknowledged, 'I've always thought there was something odd about her.'

'Well now you know,' said Andy, proud to have solved the

mystery for her. There was a lot of things she didn't know about but, fuck me, with a body like that, what did she need to know? Adrenalin surged through him as he realised he was a hair's breadth away from shagging his first bird. And what a choice way to start. Grace wasn't really black at all. Everything about her was white. Her name, her voice, even the way she walked. There was none of that cocky, swaggering lilt. She was classier than any bird he'd ever known.

'Ernie Colasanto. Well fuck me Ernie, 'ow've you bin keepin'? Last time I saw you, you was leggin' it through the school concourse wi' one a' them fuckin' addin' machines under your arm. You know they tried to do me for that. What did you want one a' them for anyway?'

Grinning sheepishly, Ernie continued assembling their order. 'Thought I'd flog it, didn't I. Some 'ope. I 'ad to chuck it in the end. Yuge bastard it was, weighed a fuckin' ton.' His eyes darted from side to side, checking that their conversation wasn't being overheard. 'Well, you don't 'ave to look very far to see 'ow I'm gettin' on. This is a right fuckin' shit'ole.'

The sparse layout and computerised cash registers indicated no chance of running a fiddle on the quiet. Behind the racks of ready-to-go food, the branch manager hovered officiously.

'Oi.' Ernie turned his attention to Grace. 'Watchew doin' with this cunt, ay? I been tellin' ya for weeks, I'm the only geezer round 'ere worth lookin' at. And now you 'ave to rub me nose in it and turn up with this cunt.' He jerked a thumb at Andy. 'I ask ya.'

'You been encouragin' 'im 'ave ya,' said Andy, joining in with the joke.

Grace maintained a dignified silence.

'That's free eighty-one,' said Ernie as he popped the apple pie into the bag along with everything else. 'How's about we all go for a drink, lunchtime tomorrow? You gonna be about?'

Andy glanced at Grace. 'Nah. Some uvver time, ay? Where you drinkin' these days anyway?'

'The Bridge Tavern on –'

'Vauxhall Bridge Road, yeah, I remember it. It's full of old paddies an' dossers, watcha wanna go there for?'

'Ahh, you ain't seen it lately, my son. They got a pool table, pinball machine, jukebox –'

'Good for birds, is it?'

'Birds? You get more talent down there in one night than you get on New Faces in an entire year.'

'Andy?' Biting a massive chunk out of her burger, Grace swallowed it down.

'You wanna watch that,' he warned. 'You get ulcers and all sorts if you don't chew your food.'

'Andy, why do you always call girls "birds"?'

'Well that's what they are,' Andy replied, sensing that she didn't care much for the word. '''S slang innit? Like boilers an' geezers. Birds an' blokes, you know?'

'Yes,' she admitted grudgingly, 'but it's, I don't know, it just sounds a bit off, that's all.'

Otto and Chrissy had conveniently departed. Grace slipped into the proverbial something more comfortable and Andy began to feel the pressure of performance bear down on him. Wank books were all right for a not-so-cheap thrill but you didn't actually learn very much. His big brother Colin's rambling fantasies were straight out of the readers' letters section and Andy was pretty sure that Colin was still a virgin. Hardly surprising, considering that he had the brain of a mongoloid and a boat race to match. Once Colin'd said that if you fucked without shooting yer load then yer balls turned blue. What if she wanted to stop halfway through? Supporting Chelsea was one thing but having your private parts sporting the club colours was going a bit over the top. What if she asked him to do something that he'd never even heard of? Like one of those funny Latin words that really means 'nostril knobbing'. Good job they'd popped into the off license on the way back, another Brew might help drown the butterflies in his stomach.

'Aww, Stan, shift yourself. I asked you to side them plates an hour since, come on chuck.' Being stuck in front of the telly watching *Coronation Street* wasn't exactly how Andy had imagined they'd be spending the rest of the evening.

'What are you thinking about?' asked Grace. She must have noticed he wasn't watching.

'Me mum.'

'What's she like?'

'She's dead. 'Er and the old man split up when I was four. I 'member goin' round Trafalgar Square on a bus wiv 'er once. Must be about the first fing I can remember. She was wearin' a white plastic mac, down to about 'ere.' Andy indicated the middle of his thigh. 'Real sixties job, know what I mean? All of a sudden the driver jams on the brakes and there's me, 'eadbuttin' the seat in front of me. Still got the scar,' he pointed to just beneath his right eyebrow.

Leaning over to look, Grace held out her hand and touched the scar lightly.

'Me mum gave the conductor a right bollockin'. Scared me, you know, but I'm glad I weren't 'im. I was bleedin' a bit, not much, but it was weird 'cos she was makin' more of a fuss than I was. Now the old man, he wouldn't a' done anyfink like that. He's more – more . . .'

'Reserved?'

'What?'

'You mean he doesn't show his emotions much.' She continued stroking the scar rhythmically.

'Not exactly, no. I mean he's got a fuckin' temper like you wouldn't believe. I 'member he used to have a go at Colin every uvver day when we was kids. One time . . .' his voice trailed away.

The weather was so hot that day, he hadn't been able to sleep a wink. The sun beat down from a clear blue sky and there wasn't the slightest breeze. The flats in Churchill Court were cold in winter but in summer they were fuckin' unbearable. The old man had started drinking at breakfast, said it cooled him down. Andy had taken a swig out of his bottle once and couldn't see how something that burned your throat could cool you down. Colin was a law unto himself. He never seemed to sweat, his dull, pale, jaundiced complexion remained unaffected by the sun and he slept through anything. Heat, cold, thunder, wind, elephants, moon rockets, atom bombs, you name it. So he was his same dopey self while everybody else was tired, sweaty and irritable. And, in the old man's case, drunk. Reaching for the tomato ketchup that he insisted on lavishing on absolutely everything, including banana sandwiches, Colin knocked the newly opened pint of Haig with his elbow and sent it skidding to the edge of the table where it teetered, for what seemed like an eternity, before toppling over and smashing on the hard floor. It's easy to tell when someone's about to hit the roof because you get those few seconds of total calm before the storm. This time the old man remained sedate for so long that Andy had almost begun to believe nothing would happen. No chance. First of all, the old man ordered him from the room. Still calm. But Andy could sense that it wouldn't be lasting much longer so he moved, sharpish. Kneeling with his eye at the keyhole, Andy vowed never to cross the old man again. Grabbing his twelve year old son by the shoulders, the old man threw Colin across the room. There was a sick clunk as Colin's head smacked against the wall and the whole flat vibrated. Half conscious, he staggered towards the old man like a punchy prize fighter. The old man whipped off his belt and Andy turned his head, looked away and put his hands over his ears.

'I know,' said Grace cheerfully, 'let's trade secrets. I'll tell you something personal about me and vice versa. I'll start.' She sat for a while, considering her first revelation. Her eyes flashed wickedly as an evidently juicy morsel came to mind. 'Okay,' she said, 'there was this boy who used to go out with my sister, Angela. I was ten at the time and he was, I don't know, fourteen perhaps. Anyway, one day he showed up at the house, this is in Peterborough, right, when there was no one there except me. I told him Angie would be back in an hour or so and he said, "Okay, I'll wait."'

'And?'

'Hold on, I'm coming to that, aren't I. Well, we're sitting on the sofa watching TV and he casually unzips his fly and gets his thing out. I didn't know where to look so I pretended not to notice and carried on watching TV. I was only ten remember.'

Silently, Andy wondered what her reaction would be now. Waiting in anticipation for Grace to finish her story, he eventually came to the realisation that she already had.

Otto's dark, introverted good looks and matching personality made Andy feel uncomfortable. Not because he disliked the bloke, it was just that Andy had never met anyone like him before. While Andy made the odd joke and rabbited on about this and that, Otto remained silent, occasionally chipping in with a simple yes or no.

'Andy's a government artist,' Grace giggled.

For the first time since he'd got back, Otto's eyes showed a flicker of interest.

'Tell him what you draw,' she said, encouraging Andy to deliver the spoiled punchline.

Though he was no Bernard Manning, Andy knew when a gag wasn't going to work. 'Nah, that's an old one, everybody's 'eard that,' he raised his voice over Grace's disappointed protests. 'I've got one that's much better. What's grey and comes in pints?' The others looked completely mystified. 'An elephant.'

Grace frowned and Otto began to chuckle. 'I don't get it,' she moaned and Otto laughed harder, 'What's an elephant got to do with it?' Otto's laughter rose in pitch.

'Does she do this a lot?' Andy inquired as he watched Grace's lips flapping in sloppy slumber.

'What? Snore?' Otto laughed. 'No, I know what you mean. Actually I've never seen her fall asleep in here before. What have you been giving her, Mandies?'

Though he was eager to know what Mandies were, Andy didn't want to show himself up. 'Nah. 'S just lager, that's all. A few Brews.'

The corners of Otto's mouth turned downwards and he raised his eyebrows. 'I'm impressed,' he said.

"Ow come?' Downing a few Brews was nothing out of the ordinary and falling asleep afterwards even less so.

'And that was really your first time?'

Andy's heart soared like a bird. For the last five minutes he'd been lying next to Grace, wondering whether he'd done it right.. The experience hadn't been anything like the one he'd imagined. It was a bit like fucking mashed potato. Grace didn't give much away either, no screaming and shouting, not even the odd grunt. And they'd been at it at least half an hour. All those stories about a quick one up against the wall, no chance. It just seemed to go on and on, really. But when Grace had taken him in her mouth, ahh well, that was when all the fuss and palaver surrounding sex had begun to make sense. What was really great was being able to watch her doing it. It was like looking at a dirty film and being in it at the same time. And when his balls began to tingle and his prick jerked reflexively, Andy had been astonished to see that she was actually *swallowing* his spunk.

'Do you like it with the light on?'

He wouldn't have had it any other way and nodded again.

'Some people just can't seem to cope with it. I prefer it, after all, once you're in the dark, you might as well be with anyone.' Running a finger along his half erect penis, Grace began massaging the tip. 'Do you want to try again?'

Could do. Why not? The thought of his pubic hair surrounding her lower face like a false beard made him hard again.

'I'll get on top,' said Grace and did just that.

Lowering his body once more, Andy let his prick slide slowly into Grace. He lay on her stomach, tired and sweating. 'Grace, are you asleep?'

She was. At last. Christ, if that was what you had to go through, no wonder married couples only did it once a fortnight.

Set well back from the main road, the apartment block was loads quieter than his own. Churchill Court was designed in such a way that, when a juggernaut thundered past, the noise would ricochet back and forth between the blocks, getting louder and louder, until eventually it reached an ear-splitting peak and gradually died away. And, if any of the lorries hit one of the numerous potholes in the road, then you could be sure that, amongst the entire total of residents, only Colin would still be asleep.

Eight

'No.' Grace whipped her arm across and slapped him hard in the face. 'Put it in the orange envelope.'

Struggling to get his bearings, Andy closed his eyes again and thought hard. What had happened yesterday? He came to see Grace and had evidently been successful. Yeah, that's right, he'd turned up really early with some Brews. Then at lunchtime Grace offered to buy some more and then . . . Ernie. They talked about having a drink with him today but how did he fit into the picture exactly? Where had they met him? Having experienced this kind of blackout before, Andy wasn't worried, it was just so frustrating. Especially since he had obviously forgotten the best bit. His throat felt dry and sandy, badly in need of a hair of the dog. The familiar gold and white design caught his eye and Andy scooped up the can of lager from the floor beside the bed. Brews were the only beer that kept their fizz overnight and he relished the thick, sweet taste, experiencing an almost immediate feeling of well being. The tension in his neck relaxed, likewise the pressure in his head and he lay back and waited for his sleeping partner to wake up.

No sooner had she pressed her hard, flat stomach against his cock than he covered it in sticky, white fluid. Shit, that wasn't meant to happen. He shrank and shrivelled in shame and Grace ran a hand along his thigh in an effort to investigate whether there was any life left in the old trouser snake. There wasn't.

'Not to worry,' she said matter-of-factly.

It only made him feel even worse. If she was so keen to have it away this morning, there was a good chance that he'd turned in a similar performance the night before. If only he could remember for sure. They lay nose to nose and he stroked her smooth, flawless forehead gently. His own forehead had been marked by three deep worry lines for the last five years. Jack used to tease him at school, saying that he looked like an old man already. The first girl he'd ever been out with said the crevices made him look intelligent. Grace's cheeks had discernible dimples and Andy slid his fingers back and forth across them. Moving her head slightly, she took two fingers into her mouth and sucked them like an ice lolly. Andy's penis began to rise automatically.

Kensington Market was bursting with colour. Every kind of stall imaginable was doing bumper business and Andy felt the old urge overtake him once more. So many people were milling about that it would be impossible for the stall owners to keep their eye on everybody.

Just inside the market, a couple of Arabs were selling plain sweatshirts, jumpers and jeans. Nothing flash, just good quality merchandise. Examining the thick khaki sweaters, Grace bought one for Damien, her younger brother. There were four siblings in her family and, as she already had presents for her parents, that left three to go. But the Arabs were on the case and, while one of them served Grace, the other kept his eye on Andy.

Next stop was the basement where Grace explained about all the drug paraphernalia. She didn't approve of drugs, in fact, that was part of the reason why she and Otto had split up. By the time he'd finished smoking, snorting and swallowing he was of absolutely no use to anyone. Of course, she dropped the odd blue every now and again but . . . Christ, yeah, Andy had forgotten all about his introduction to speed.

Exactly as Jack had forecast, a strange feeling of acceleration had shot through Andy as the number eleven meandered through World's End. Each thought that came into his head was even more thrilling than the last and suddenly he felt desperate to do something. He couldn't just sit there while precious seconds ticked away. There were plans to be made, work to be done, why if he put his mind to it, anything was possible. World fuckin' domination even. Earlier on, he had been a bit miffed when Jack announced that he had a rehearsal to go to but now all Andy wanted to do was get down to Bishop's, plonk himself on his favourite bench and formulate his master plan. Wheels. That was what he needed more than anything else. This time, however, he wasn't thinking of doing a spot of TDA and going for a joy ride. No, this time it would be kosher and above board. He needed a motor, some lessons and licence. But most of all he needed funds. One decent job, that's all it would take. If he kept his ear to the ground maybe he'd hear a few whispers about who was holding the folding in Churchill Court these days. It wasn't until the following day that he realised it would be a year before he was legally old enough to drive a car.

'All right, Anthea love,' Andy gushed in his best Bruce Forsyth, 'give us a twirl.'

Shaking her head, Grace shrugged and took off the jacket.

'Wha–? It looks ace, wassa matter?'

She tapped the small white cardboard price tag discreetly attached to the black leather cuff.

Okay, that was the one. Andy checked himself in the mirror. His gun-metal blue Crombie coat hung on his skinny frame as though it were still waiting to be collected by its owner. Plenty of room in there. Returning the jacket to the rack, Grace wandered over to the counter. Andy slipped the jacket off its hanger and whisked it under his coat. Putting his right hand in his coat pocket, he hugged the stolen article against his leg and sidled up to Grace. 'Let's go.'

'What? Why, what's the hurry,' she said, more loudly than he would have liked.

''Ave you finished up 'ere? Shall we go?' Inclining his head towards the door, Andy wordlessly urged her to leave with him. *Now*.

'Wait a minute,' she protested and grabbed his rigid right arm,

'I'm looking at something.' He pulled away stiffly. 'What's the . . . ?'

'These, love?' Behind the counter a tough-looking skinhead wearing a fresh number one and tasty loafers, jerked and shuffled actively in time to the ska tune blasting out from a mysteriously hidden source. He had an abrasive Glaswegian accent and ominous, blue tinted National Health glasses. This geezer was 'ard as fuckin' nails. With ten like him you could nobble any firm in London. Black or white. The skin picked out a baby-sized black leather wristband covered in evil looking, rust coloured studs from the glass topped cabinet in front of him.

'What are they?' asked Grace.

'Cock straps.'

'And this?'

Fishing out what looked like a lead weight, Grace swung the dense pyramid by its long leather strap.

Glancing over at Andy, the skin shifted into top gear and began punching the air with his arms like twin pistons. Andy tried to appear to relax his right side, without actually doing so. 'What is it you're looking for exactly?' asked the skin, not bothering to answer Grace's question or even look at her.

'Nothing really, just browsing,' she replied.

Behind his blue lenses, the skin's eyes locked onto Andy's. 'Uh huh,' he panted, dealing out a double dose of grievous bodily harm to the imaginary man in front of him. 'What about your friend here?' he asked her while still staring at Andy. 'What's his preference?' He laughed abruptly and turned back towards her. 'Perhaps there's something you're after that isn't on display?'

On the wall behind him, a series of white T-shirts were pinned up. Each one had a different design but they all depicted orgy scenes, although who was doing what to whom remained unclear. One thing though, there didn't seem to be many birds. Andy refocused. There didn't seem to be *any* birds. Looking away from the T-shirts he noticed the corner of the skin's mouth twitch upwards.

'Poppers?' Grace breathed excitedly.

'Seven a bottle.' The skinhead held his thumb and forefinger a couple of inches apart. In a flash, two crisp blue notes had come between them. Depositing the notes into the till, the skin handed a fistful of change to Grace. 'Have a nice day,' he winked and they left, not a moment too soon.

Dragging Grace behind him with his free arm, Andy weaved out of the market, along Kensington High Street and round the first available corner. He didn't know this area very well and it made him nervous. Hurriedly, he handed her his Crombie and slipped into the leather jacket.

'Oh my God,' Grace's jaw hung as though she had a bad cold and could no longer breathe through her nose. She passed him his coat and folded her arms haughtily. 'Is this the way you normally carry on?' she snapped, 'Helping yourself to anything that takes your fancy?'

'Merry Christmas,' he chuckled as he buttoned the Crombie.

'As soon as the top's off, put the bottle directly beneath your nostrils and breathe in as hard as you can. The liquid evaporates really quickly so you've got to be fast.'

'What's it do?' Andy asked apprehensively. Amyl nitrate, he didn't like the sound of that at all. Not at all. 'Here,' he said, passing the phial back to Grace, 'after you.'

Screwing off the cap she shoved the neck of the bottle into one nostril, held the other with her finger and inhaled deeply. 'Okay,' she hissed and held out the open bottle.

The bus jerked violently and he snatched the phial before it had time to spill and rammed it up his nose. At first the effect was similar to smelling salts, a sharp, stinging vapour. Suddenly he was hurtling downwards in free fall.

Returning to the flat, they found it empty. They lounged in front of an old black and white movie on TV.

'What was it like inside?' Grace inquired gingerly.

He'd been wondering when she was going to get around to asking that question, everybody did.

'Watcha wanna know?'

Phil the Greek ran East Wing. The other lads called him that because no one could pronounce his surname. He was a fair bloke, lenient almost. The proof of that came the day he explained to Andy what it meant to be a Greek Cypriot and reminded him that there were two Turkish Cypriots in East Wing. But they received exactly the same treatment as anyone else. It cost two bob a week to keep Phil sweet and whatever he asked you to do, you did it. He once asked Andy to lay his hand on the table and splay his fingers. Then he proceeded to jab a small pen knife into the spaces between Andy's fingers moving backwards and forwards, getting faster and faster. Sooner or later, Andy realised, he was going to miss and the certainty of that fact brought him an almost hypnotic calm. Even the screws liked Phil the Greek, he kept bovver down to a minimum. Most of the lads got rid of their aggression during the strenuous exercise routines. That was the weird thing about Borstal, you came out twice as hard as when you went in. Plus, the mistake that put you in there could be explained and corrected by someone who had more experience. Andy picked up tips on everything from lock-picking to queer-bashing.

She laughed. It was as though she had punched a hole through the wall of his stomach and ripped his guts out. Why did it hurt so much? Slag. He wanted to knock her black carcass halfway across the fucking room. The request had been simple enough. Could he go to Peterborough with her? Christ, it was nothing compared to what Jack was up to. At first Grace had asked what for and when he answered she laughed. Sticks and stones may break my bones . . . bullshit. It was the most unpleasant feeling he'd ever had. Ever. Andy wanted to get back at her, badly. Ssssuperbadly. But the most obvious line of attack stuck in his craw like a chicken bone. His cheeks ached in a fixed false smile and he relaxed his face but the worst was yet to come. Gazing at him with her soft brown eyes, Grace understood that she had hurt him. She opened her mouth as if to speak but no words came out.

Andy felt his anger subside suddenly. 'Bit of a wally idea, that,' he laughed, 'I can just imagine what my old man would say if I brought you 'ome for Christmas.'

'Will it be just the three of you?' she asked softly.

'Yeah. Free Masons in one 'ouse is more than enough, I can tell ya. Last year we 'ad the law round, no joke,' he assured her in reaction to Grace's expression of incredulity. 'There's this bir–' he cut himself short and smiled, 'this girl 'oo lives in the flat below, a right prick teaser. Anyway, it's about four o'clock on Boxin' Day mornin' and the old man says – 'e's pissed as a fart, right – the old man says, "I'm gonna take a look at 'er downstairs." Me and Colin are sittin' there, not exactly sober, laughin' our 'eads off, thinkin' that 'e's gonna go down there and show 'imself up. 'Alf a minute later, 'e comes back with this Black and Decker – what 'e never uses – plugs it into the wall, rolls back the carpet and starts drillin' fru' the fuckin' floor.'

'Didn't you try to stop him?'

'Stop 'im? On my life, it was the funniest fuckin' fing I've ever seen.'

The next train to Peterborough was due to leave in five minutes. That was British Rail terminology for approximately half an hour. Grace and Andy sat drinking tea in the drably anonymous station bar.

'You're mad,' Andy asserted, shaking his head in amazement.

'I don't see why,' Grace retorted, 'I'm not breaking any laws am I?'

'No, but the money's yours. You're legally entitled to it. You must've walked away from over a grand already!'

'Yes, well, when you put it like that . . .' Her voice trailed away and Grace frowned. 'I'd still rather not ever have to go in one of those places, after all you n–'

"Oo d'you 'ate most in the entire world?'

'Brooke Shields. But wh–?'

'Right. So if I said "do you wanna meet this Brooke Shields geezer th–'

'She's a she.'

'Yeah? All right anyway, if I s–'

'I'd say yes, just so that I'd have the chance to spit in her eye,' Grace grinned maliciously. 'Look Andy, I know what you're getting at but I just don't like the idea, okay?'

'It takes five minutes,' he persisted. 'You sign your name once a week and, for that, you get twenty-five notes a week. You've nothin' to lose.'

Except perhaps your patience.

Swinging her chair at the glass partition, the woman screamed with fury. A distinct improvement on her earlier unaccompanied rendition of 'Hey Joe', complete with simulated feedback guitar solo. She was Australian by the sound of it and nutty as a fruitcake. Breaking off from his explanation of why her unemployment benefit had been curtailed, the man behind the enquiries counter dived reflexively as the chair bounced off the thick, reinforced glass and clattered to the floor. The tubby security guard had buggered off somewhere and Andy rubbed his hands with glee. Although the woman had no way of getting to the man behind the counter, she was evidently going to die trying. For a moment Andy had been disappointed to see her back away from the partition. The man resumed his normal position and adjusted his tie. Abruptly the woman charged forward, jumped up onto her side of the counter and spat through the wire mesh above the glass. She rattled the wire and kicked the glass like a caged animal. It was the man's job to stay put and he did so under a shower of saliva and verbal abuse.

Andy's spontaneous Xmas gift was a perfect match for the black leather trousers that Grace already owned and together they looked a treat. The urge to get on the train with her came over him again and he fought it off with some difficulty. Standing on the crowded King's Cross platform, they kissed. Lapping at his tongue with her own, she seemed to be drinking his saliva. Leather rustled and squeaked as she hugged him tighter and rubbed her pelvis against his leg.

'Come on,' he said and grabbed her arm.

'Wha–?' Grace gasped as he jumped onto the train and heaved her aboard. 'Look Andy, I told you there's no –'

'In 'ere,' Andy snapped, indicating the washroom door. Pushing her inside, he slammed the door and locked it.

'Here?' she asked apprehensively.

Andy replied by unzipping his fly.

'But there's no time, you'll get unnhh . . .'

Blood raged in his cock and Grace's gaze fixed on it hungrily. All at once she sank to her knees. 'You'd better be quick.' Seizing his prick, she shoved it into her mouth and dragged her teeth roughly along its length. A low moan became audible, and, after a few seconds, Andy realised that he was the source of the sound. Gripping his buttocks hard, Grace bobbed her head rhythmically. Andy felt himself beginning to come and kneaded the back of her head with his fingers. Doors began to slam as the guard moved along the train, making his final check before blowing the whistle. Andy looked down to see Grace slip a hand underneath the waistband of her trousers. The beads in her hair clacked cacophonously and the blasts of hot air from her nose became more frequent. His whole body convulsed and he accidentally pulled out of her mouth. Jets of spunk shot into her face and eyes and she rocked back and forth on her haunches, clawing at her crotch with both hands. Licking at the spunk like a thirsty animal, Grace grimaced and froze. There was a shrill, piercing whistle and she sagged and fell into a crumpled heap on the floor.

As the train pulled out of the station a fog of doubts and fears began to descend in Andy's mind. Like a mouse running around his own tiny treadmill, it was great fun to begin with but now he wanted to get off. If only she were white. But she wasn't even brown, she was black. As the ace of spades. Everything was falling apart at the seams and there was no one to turn to for advice. He wondered what his mother would have said. Though they hadn't been close, he'd always liked her a lot. After she left the old man, she married again and her second husband was an all right geezer. And Susan, his daughter, was exactly what a little girl should be. Shy, delicate and sensitive.

'Could Andrew Mason please go straight to the headmistress's office. Andrew Mason.' The speaker on the wall in the corner of the classroom clicked off.

'Story a' my fuckin' life,' Andy grinned and rose from the desk. "Ere look after this, will ya,' he said and slipped Jack the master key that opened ninety per cent of the doors in the school. As Andy loped down the aisle towards the classroom door, Jack hummed the death march ominously. The school concourse had been empty except for one gangling grotesque, hovering like a vulture. As Andy approached the figure, he put on his guilty, hunted look. The first rule of teacher-pupil tactical warfare was to keep the enemy off balance.

'Mason.' The vulture waved him over and sighed with detached disdain. 'All right Mason, where are you supposed to be?'

"Ere, sir,' Andy offered cheerfully.

'Any more cheek from you lad and I'll knock your ruddy block off.'

Having exhausted his ration of kid glove treatment some time ago, Andy was used to being physically threatened and he looked forward to the day when one of those threats was carried out. Whichever teacher was foolish enough to do that, wouldn't know what had hit him. Or her. 'Whose class are you skiving off from, boy?'

'Nobody's.'

Grasping his blazer collar, the vulture began dragging Andy along the concourse. 'I've had just about enough of you, boy. I think it's time you saw the headmistress.'

'I'm sorry that you've wasted your time, Mr Algy. I presume Andrew failed to tell you he was already on his way to see me.'

The veins on the vulture's temples began to stand out.

'Yeah, sorry about that,' Andy smirked, 'but you didn't give me much chance did you, Mr Orgy?' There was a fine line between the pronunciation of 'Algy' and 'orgy' and Andy maintained constant duty on the wrong side of it. The muscles in Mr Algy's jaw flexed as he shot a vicious glance at Andy before walking away. The sensation of wanting to laugh but not being able to was thrilling.

'You'd better come in,' said Mrs Green in a tone of voice that did not bode well. Andy made a quick mental résumé of the possible reasons for this summons. Top of the list would have to be the bomb threats. Since the IRA had blown away half the ticket collector's face at Pimlico tube station, everybody in the area was on their guard. And so, when Jack launched into one of his endless gripes about how much he hated the art class on Tuesday afternoons, Andy suggested that, as there was no other way of getting out of it, they evacuate the entire building. Second on the list would be the fire in the boys' cloakroom. Andy still wasn't quite sure what had happened there. One minute they were having a friendly game of poker and a smoke and then suddenly the whole fucking place was alight. According to Jack it was something to do with the polystyrene in the seats. That and the fact that Andy had tried to stub his fag out on one of them. Third on the list was the graffiti. A couple of birds in the third year had been caught touching each other up and the news spread like wildfire. Helped enormously by the slogans sprayed on almost every available wall in the school. Although they'd been very careful to disguise their handwriting both he and Jack realised they were bound to be blamed, sooner or later. After all, not one of the other two thousand pupils had the guts to pull a stunt like that.

'It's about your step-sister, Susan Mallinder.'

'Sue? Is she all right?'

'I'm afraid we've had some rather bad news. We've tried to reach her father but we h–'

'He's away.' In Belgium. His step-father was a brickie and worked wherever he could.

'Are there any other relations we could contact? Perhaps *your* mother ... You see, Mrs Mallinder passed away this morning.' Mallinder? But Sue's real mum had re-married; she was Mrs Norris now.

A big, fat syringe stuck in the base of Andy's spine and began to suck the life out of him.

'I'm dreadfully sorry. You obviously knew her well.'

'Not really.'

Prising the back off his transistor radio, Andy extracted two tenners from behind the batteries. It was twenty-five past six and he had plenty of time to get the old man's and Colin's presents before they got back from the pub.

I speak a one dread, seh show me ya natty dread. So the dread flash 'im locks an' a lightnin' clap an' a weak 'eart drop. The deejay's cocky tenor toasted over a rolling rockers rhythm, Channel One style, well hard. A group of blacks huddled around a small pile of notes and coins in the corner of the courtyard. A bright red ghetto blaster handled the subsonic, grumbling bass surprisingly well, given its small size.

'Wanna game?' Yogi looked up from his hand of cards and smiled. The truce between his crew and the skins had lasted well, so far. Everybody was aware that it couldn't go on forever but, for the moment, the mutual distrust remained unspoken. When the hand finished, Andy sat in.

'Stud poker, four cards up, one down. Deuces wild and remember, a flush beats a straight.' All eyes turned to Big Adrian and everybody laughed, including him. It was amazing he could be so good humoured about it, after all, having his nostril slashed wide open by an angry gambling opponent's flick-knife can't have been much fun. The scar was so well defined it looked as though his nose could open up again any minute.

'It's five to be in,' said Yogi as he dealt the down card to each player, 'that's the minimum, sky's the limit.'

Andy felt the two ten pound notes crinkle in his trouser pocket. He was only too well aware that, now he was in the game, the possibility of losing all his money was quite likely.

Chewing a matchstick tentatively, Yogi narrowed his eyes as he dealt Andy his first up card. The two of diamonds, Andy's heart sang until Yogi dealt himself the two of hearts and immediately raised Andy's initial bet of ten pence to a quid. Next up for Andy was the ace of diamonds and, as there were now only two people in the game, the others descended into hushed excitement. 'Possible running flush,' Yogi announced and dealt himself the six of clubs. 'Pair of aces to bet.' Andy upped it to one fifty and Yogi nodded. At the end of the deal, the pot had reached well over ten pounds. More like fifteen. Andy examined his opponent's cards closely. The eight of hearts and the seven of spades gave Yogi a great shot at a straight. It was possible he already had it. Yogi eyed his down card casually. No, if he had it, he wouldn't need to look. With three aces up, including the wild deuce, Andy decided to make it interesting. 'No change,' he said and exchanged his tenner for a fiver in the pot. As expected, Yogi changed his down card and momentarily stopped chewing his matchstick. He had it. 'I raise you another five,' he taunted and sent another tenner fluttering onto the pile. Andy slipped off his watch. 'Thirty.' It was worth more than a hundred. 'Seen.' Yogi tossed another twenty-five quid into the pot and flipped over his down card confidently, expecting Andy to have no more than a full house.

As Andy bounced down to the off licence, he went over the game in his head. By the time the deal had finished, Andy already knew he'd won, with three aces showing and a hidden fourth. Just as he was about to change his queen, in a superfluous attempt to get five of a kind, he realised that, by staying with his original cards, he would automatically lead Yogi to believe he had an easily beatable full house. Poor sod. Andy had once lost a similar amount and he knew that crushing sense of defeat. Heh heh. A car load of long-haired drunks flew past on the opposite side of the road, vociferously reminding anyone who cared to listen that tomorrow was Christmas Day. Owen Brookes Estate stood tall and foreboding to Andy's left and he began taking longer strides, the best way to walk quickly without appearing to be scared. Wogs, like dogs, could smell fear and on this particular estate they were the majority rather than the minority. The Owen Brookes crews made Yogi's lot look like something out of Enid Blyton. But the off licence was built into the front of the estate and getting to it was worth the risk, given Gerald's dirt cheap prices. Gerald was a South London lad and what he lacked in muscle he made up for in pure fat. He was twenty stone if he was an ounce and, apart from a few bricks thrown through the shop window, he'd never had any bovver. Now the window was boarded up and colourful slogans and murals covered the hardboard making the shop look more like an amusement arcade. Gerald and his wife Pat lived above the shop. They had a two-year-old son who was mentally retarded and the tension this caused was never very far from the surface of Pat's perennially bruised and battered face.

'So I sez to 'im, I sez there's no point in comin' round 'ere, you randy so and so, I sez, 'cos you won't get nuffink from me.' Brenda folded her arms underneath her tits, pushing them up until they seemed to be pointing at the ceiling. Licking his lips lasciviously, Gerald eyed the well-rounded twelve-year-old like a punter in a brothel. Brenda had already acquired the nickname Superslag and she'd probably end up on the streets. Everybody had their own variation on the 'when Brenda gave me a blow job' boast, including Andy but, as he'd lied to save face, he knew there was a good chance that none of the stories were actually true. But if she started selling tickets, Gerald would undoubtedly be first in the queue.

'Ev'nin' my son, watchew 'avin'?' Gerald turned his attention away from Brenda, who'd obviously only popped in for a chinwag. 'Aye aye, wassis then, you won the pools or summink?' he asked in response to Andy's request for two bottles of Glen-fiddich, eight Brews, eight Newke Browns, a packet of Henri Wintermans half coronas and a large tin of Quality Street.

'On my life, you wouldn't a' believed it,' Andy beamed and proceeded to relay the whole hand in glorious detail. As he reached the climax of the story, Gerald was nearly as excited as Andy had been at the time of playing. Behind him, Brenda rustled and shuffled in an immature attempt to feign lack of interest.

'You must feel on top a' the bleedin' world,' Gerald chuckled as he packed the booze into two plastic carrier bags.

'*My* dad won a couple of 'undred on the 'orses last week,' Brenda whined, apparently missing the point that it was Andy who had won the money, not his old man. They both ignored her.

Nine

It was Christmas Eve, so the choice of records at Chrissy's disposal was depressingly limited. Like every other radio station in the country, the key word at the moment was 'seasonal'. It was the time of year that totally justified Jack's constant, ranting criticism of the music business. The record companies stopped pretending to be mild-mannered patrons of the arts and revealed themselves to be . . . Supercon!

Switching to channels three and four, Chrissy monitored the next commercial break on her headphones whilst John Lennon tried to remind everybody what was really going on. Satisfied that the cassette was properly cued, she faded the ex-Beatle and let rip with an ad for skin cream.

'Oh no, Trace, look at my face. It's covered in spots.' 'Don't worry, Sharon, I've got just the thing. Here.' 'Invigel? That's new. But does it work?' A shimmering harp faded into an incongruous male voice. 'With Christmas just around the corner –' They'd actually been running the ad since the second week in October. '– most of us can be sure of one thing. Eating too much rich food is a sure fire way of upsetting the body's delicate balance of chemicals, often producing unwanted patches of dry or greasy skin. But now, new Invigel –' Again with the harp, already. '– with its specially formulated built-in moisturiser, treats each pore individually, soothing away irritation. Why, in just three days, *you* can see the difference. Let's see how Sharon is getting on.' Zzzzingggg. 'Hi, Trace. Good party last night, wannit?' 'Yeah. You looked great, new Invigel really works. And who was that hunky guy you were with? He's a dream.' 'Gary? Oh he's just a friend.' Harpo and Groucho returned once more. 'Conclusive proof that new – zzzingg – Invigel really works. New – zzzinggg – Invigel. It really works.'

Despite herself, Chrissy had given in to the brainwashing bombardment and bought a tube. The acne that had waylaid her in the sixth form had never completely cleared up. And Invigel didn't *really* work.

'And now, as we slip into the final hour of the show, I'd like to take this opportunity to remind you about the rest of the day's entertainment here on LWS. Coming up at three o'clock we have . . .' Putting her mouth onto automatic pilot, Chrissy let her mind wander, and it came to rest on Otto. She tried to think of something else. Rounding off her spiel, Chrissy cued in another record. 'As you're probably aware, I don't normally do dedications but on this particular occasion I've decided to make an exception. If you've ever been in love with somebody but, for whatever reason, have been unable to let them know, then this is for you. "My Eyes Adored You".' Violins soared and sighed behind Frankie Valli's warm, honeyed crooning. His voice had really changed since the 'Rag Doll' days. Then it had been a high pitched, androgynous whine, perfectly suited for sending little girls into squeals of delight. Chrissy could still remember the first time she heard Elvis's nervous, shaking vibrato on 'Heartbreak Hotel'. Hearing him stutter and yelp from the transistor hidden beneath her pillow was like having him right there in bed with her. Now that really would have been something. 'American singing star caught in Halifax love nest with underage girl.' No, perhaps not. If she had one regret about those times, it was that Nat had been too old to be a proper sister. At first it was like having two mothers, which was pretty horrendous, and then suddenly Nat was gone. Those four years of looking after Phyllis, until she was old enough to leave home, had been murder. And re-running those ghastly memories was a pastime she would gladly replace with indecent fantasies of Otto. She tried to think of something else.

At six o'clock every Sunday evening, Chrissy used to call Phyllis without fail. And then one day the draining futility of their attempts to communicate with each other had proved too much. Screaming as loud as her lungs would allow, she slammed the phone down and smashed a glass of tomato juice against the wall. Now, there was only one day on which that chore had to be performed and this just happened to be it. Christmas Eve, Phyllis's birthday. Pacing anxiously around the kitchen floor, Chrissy decided to do some washing-up first.

After half an hour, and a considerable amount of sweat, the previous fortnight's clinging remains clung no more. Stacking away the last of the plates, she turned to look at the phone. Its original creamy hue had yellowed through years of use and it was time somebody gave it a thorough going over. Armed with a piece of old dress material and a can of furniture polish, she soon had the phone spotless and gleaming. In fact the rest of the room looked positively dull by comparison.

When all the surfaces had been wiped down, Chrissy made a momentous decision. She was going to – wait for it – *clean the grill!* As she never gave dinner parties, the small, single level grill suited her cooking needs perfectly and it had given her five years' impeccable service. And now Harry, the grill, was being rewarded with the bath of a lifetime. Using a knife as a chisel and the heel of her palm as a hammer, Chrissy set to work. The trouble with Harry was that it was difficult to differentiate between him and the burnt, black gunk that coated him. The knife scraped and screamed across the metal, making Chrissy grit her teeth and shiver. Tiny black shavings fluttered to the floor and, by the time Dirty Harry had metamorphosed into Flash Harry, Chrissy had nominated hoovering as her next major task. The vacuum cleaner's roaring wheeze was like a thousand dentist's drills buzzing into her skull. She'd forgotten how much she hated that sound. She switched it off quickly. In an effort to avoid Phyllis, she was now behaving exactly like her. There was nothing for it but to pick up the phone.

'Chrissy? It is you, isn't it? I'm so bloody glad you've called. Wow, I've got a friend in the world, you know what I mean?'

'Why, what's happened?' asked Chrissy worriedly. This was not the same Julia she had spoken to in the summer. That Julia had been as cocky and arrogant as ever. You knew where you were with the old Julia. 'Why aren't you at home?' Although Julia worked like a packhorse, Chrissy hadn't really expected her to be in the office on Christmas Eve.

'I've left Bashi. I couldn't stand it any longer. The insults, the constant suspicion that I was screwing around. Every time I looked over my shoulder he was there, breathing down my neck. He's got no right. No bloody right at all,' Julia blustered with pompous outrage.

She'd been screwing around all right. Poor old Bashi. 'What about the boy?'

'Oh, he'll be fine with his dad. I'm not worried about him, I'm worried about me. There are three parties tonight at which I'm obliged to make an appearance –' Her proper, middle-class voice bristled with pride. ' –and I'll be damned if I'm going to let that obnoxious little oik ruin it for me. Please come with me, Chris, I need someone to lean on, please?' The change in her tone was so dramatic it was surprising she hadn't taken to the stage years ago. Bette Davis eat your heart out.

Chrissy made her apologies and hung up. Perhaps having a child set you free from the maternal instinct. For the first time in their friendship, Chrissy felt dislike for Julia. Not an easily definable, overall dislike but a thin, spiky feeling of mistrust and uneasiness. How could she do it? A two-year-old mind was like putty in the hands of its parents. Every word said, every deed done was filed away in the 'Top Priority' drawer of the infant's memory. 1975 Mummy and Daddy say 'hello'. 1976 begin to be able to say 'hello' back. 1977 Mummy says 'goodbye'. Charming. What a foundation for future confidence. Bashi was a kind man but he was still only a man. It wasn't enough. Perhaps if the child had been a girl – no – that would have made it even worse. Chrissy began to wonder whether her own child would be a boy or a girl. And then she began to wonder whether it would ever be.

'Eeyah! You're Christine McArfur, untcha?'

Perfect. Slap bang in the middle of Sainsbury's. Busiest day of the year.

'Oi. Over eeyah. Look. Issat bird on telly.'

Whatever happened to good old British reserve? It was never there, that's what happened to it. We're just as vulgar, pushy and loutish as everybody else. Chrissy's fame was moderate but she'd been shopping here for six months. Why now? If she were Jimmy Savile, fair enough. But this lecherous, red-nosed scum of the earth was using her to attract attention to himself. Like a leech, he was sucking her dry. Remember the golden rule. Imagine you aren't the person people think you are. How would you react?

Chrissy smiled inanely and gazed around the supermarket to see if anyone else was crazy enough to think that she was really *her*. 'It's funny you know, you're the second one today. It's the new hair-do, au naturel. All the stars have it, you know. When they're at home. Relaxing. Or whatever.'

Fury flashed across the man's face and then it was gone. He knew he was right and he also knew that no one else believed him. The game was over and he had lost.

Large packs of bacon off-cuts were on special offer, half price. Chrissy bought two for the price of one.

'Could you possibly pass me one of those, please?' An energetic, round-faced young woman stood with both hands holding a pile of groceries, the top of which was crammed underneath her chin. 'I thought you were marvellous back there, very efficient.' The woman's intelligent, probing eyes indicated no chance of another bluff. 'I didn't bother to get a basket because I didn't think I'd need one.' She grunted gratefully as Chrissy slipped the packet of bacon under her chin. 'It's the only meat worth eating these days. You can't pretend to be a slice of bacon. You either are one, or you're not.' She shrugged her shoulders. 'Are you a meat-eater?'

'No.'

'No, I thought not.'

After dumping the shopping back at the flat, Chrissy went for a walk. One of the nicest things about living in Parson's Green was there was a lovely park nearby. She'd done this walk so many times she could probably do it with her eyes closed. Weaving her way through the back streets toward Putney Bridge, she closed her eyes. Although every lamppost, tree and paving stone was indelibly etched into her memory, she lost all confidence and opened them again. It was strange to think that, were she permanently blind, it would have been a doddle. There were so many things that could be done when there was no other choice.

Long ago she had given up feeling guilty about moving into such an affluent community. Stockbrokers, doctors and deejays all fell into the same category at the end of the day. You worked hard, but no harder than a lot of other people who, by some quirk of fate, were paid only a fraction of what you earned. And if your conscience really meant that much to you, how did you stop feeling guilty? Mother Theresa probably slept well at night but who wanted to spend the rest of their life amongst poverty and disease? And if everybody did give up their worldly possessions and heeded the cause. . . ? Unfortunately the answer to that would never change and Chrissy felt glad that she'd given up feeling guilty about it.

One out of every ten houses seemed to have construction work being done to it. Interesting to note how the wolf-whistle had gone into decline recently. There would always be a few mumbled chuckles of camaraderie amongst the builders but the outward gestures and shouts of 'gerremoff' seemed to have ceased. She remembered the verbal put-down Julia had given a young brickie on the Earl's Court Road.

'Oi darlin', gis' ya phone numbah. I'll come rahnd and give you one. You look like you could do wiv a good shaggin'.' The boy must have taken lessons from Noël Coward. Julia stopped dead. 'Which one of us are you interested in?' 'Makes no odds to me darlin'.' 'Well I certainly wouldn't want to have sex with a Neanderthal mollusc like you. How about you, Chris?'

Bishop's Park ran along the edge of the Thames, overlooking the river's murky grey expanse. Supermarket trolleys, Wellington boots and human corpses were regularly found bobbing around in there. People would throw themselves off Wandsworth Bridge, why Wandsworth God only knew, and float upstream to Putney. The very idea of plunging into that filthy blackness was a nightmare in itself, regardless of the risk of drowning. Although Chrissy had been known to manage a length or two in Putney Baths, the sea and its myriad off-shoots were another thing entirely.

Late afternoon traffic buzzed lazily across Putney Bridge as Chrissy wandered down to the other end of the park. On her way, she passed a woman wheeling a twin push-chair. It was empty. The sky was clear and a biting wind blew in from the Thames. Thrusting her hands deep into her coat pockets, Chrissy bowed her head. At the far end of the park the floodlights in Fulham football ground towered into the air. A plane rumbled overhead and from this angle it looked as though it was about to collide with one of the gargantuan metal structures. Barbed wire ran along the top of the wall of the ground making it look like a maximum security prison. This was where the male of the species could behave like an animal, except that where animals had pride and dignity, football supporters had Dutch courage and bigotry. Mind you, Fulham fans were quite reserved compared with their Chelsea counterparts who weren't content to restrict the violence to inside the ground. The fact that Martin wore spectacles hadn't stopped him from receiving a vicious beating in broad daylight on the Fulham Road. He didn't even *like* football.

Ten

The ride home was a long but comfortable one. Uncle Max was very proud of his new Cadillac and wanted to take it easy until the engine had been properly broken in. Central Philadelphia was split into two, he explained, the old and the new. Five minutes out of the bus station, brownstone buildings and worn concrete roads made the place look like a gigantic set for a 1930s' gangster movie. This was the old. Max was a veterinary surgeon. He had a wife and one son. These were the only details Jack could remember clearly, everything else being a blur at best.

'Heyja. Good to see. Heard all about. Do you want to?'

Jack smiled and frowned simultaneously. 'Sorry?'

'Oh, heh heh,' Max beamed. 'I bet you'll be. Joanne's making. I love it when. She says I'm a pig. Heh heh.' Max bobbed and weaved as though dodging an invisible adversary.

He was utterly charming and the peculiar way his voice trailed off at the end of each sentence made him even more so.

'I must admit, I'm famished,' Jack agreed, not knowing quite what Joanne was making but sensing it would be delicious.

Gradually the old town gave way to a vast expanse of nothingness. They glided silently along a wide, straight road for what seemed like hours, the inky blackness of the night unwilling to give the slightest hint as to their whereabouts. A strange light hung in the sky, too colourful to be a star, too static to be an aeroplane. It wasn't until the light was directly above the car, and Max swerved gently to the right, that Jack realised it was a traffic signal, suspended far above the road. Tall hedgerows did a shadowy dance on either side of the Caddy's headlights. At ten p.m. on Christmas Eve it seemed as though the entire suburban population of Philadelphia was asleep.

As he trotted up the steps after Max, the first thing Jack noticed was the number on the front door. 7019. That meant there must be about ten thousand houses in this one street alone. The second thing Jack noticed was being knocked flat on his back by an hysterical dwarf, screaming at the top of his voice.

'Jack, Jack, Jack, are you gonna show me how to play da drums? Huh? Are you, Jack? Are you? Buddle uddle uddle uddle.' Tiny clenched fists beat lightly on Jack's chest and a round, fat face leaned into his own, grinning. Saliva dribbled from his attacker's mouth, splashing into Jack's eye and he recoiled.

'Joey, stop that at once,' a woman's voice rang out sharply as the poison dwarf scrambled up Jack's chest preparing, no doubt, to dispatch another liquid missile, 'I said *stop* that.' Abruptly, the weight on his chest was gone and Jack got to his feet. Joanne held her son, kicking, waving and squawking in mid-air, while Max chortled quietly to himself. 'I'm sorry,' she wheezed with some effort, 'I told the boy he could stay up to meet you, but Joey . . . well, Joey's Joey.' The dimples in her cheeks deepened in a tired smile. 'Come in, come in, you must be hungry.'

So far, the only physical feature that seemed to connect these people was their rotundness. Max, like his brother Ben, Jack's father, was tall, balding and bearded. He wore an off-the-peg, two-piece suit with, unfortunately, flared trousers and a white shirt straining, almost audibly, around his more than ample girth. As Joanne led the way into a cosy kitchen-cum-dining room her huge hips swung majestically from side to side in a smooth, flowing movement. How come black people still look good when they're fat? Jack wondered as he watched Max galumphing along behind his wife. Joanne was black in a way that Grace, with her 'I've just come from my ballet class', poker-up-the-arse gait, was not. Though Joanne was the lighter skinned of the two, she had a sassy, fatback quality. Max was a lucky man.

According to Ben, when they first married things had not been easy. The liberalism of the late sixties had yet to have any effect on the closeted narrow mindedness of the local inhabitants. Max's flourishing veterinary practice took a sudden nose dive as word spread that the avenue was playing host to its first non-caucasian resident. There were no Nazi pyrotechnics, just a subtle, insidious turning up of the collective nose. But Max continued to go to the golf club and Joanne went on sending dinner party invitations to their neighbours and, after a couple of demoralising, soul-destroying years, the ice slowly began to thaw. Whenever Ben talked about his brother his eyes would moisten with nostalgia and his voice thicken with pride and emotion. Max was a gentle giant, quietly self-effacing, doggedly determined and a thoroughly good man.

'Ohh this is just. Jack, have you ever? I'm going to.' Bobbing and weaving about in his chair at the dining table, Max grinned sheepishly and popped another huge slice of cake into his mouth.

'Every year he says "next year I'm gonna get rid of this belly" and every year it gets a little bigger,' Joanne sighed good naturedly. 'You better have some more, Jack, before he finishes the whole thing.'

Jack's stomach gurgled in protest. 'I couldn't manage another morsel. It was great.'

'You see how easy it is to say "no"?' Joanne declared, watching the penultimate slice of thick, gooey chocolate cake disappear into her husband's gaping oral orifice. 'You wouldn't believe it but he used to be as skinny as you.'

Skinny was not a word often used to describe Jack's muscly, medium build but it seemed close enough, given his present company. Joey had been packed off to bed with the promise that yes, of course Santa would still be coming despite Jack's unexpected presence in the house.

'I'd better get the. We don't want the little. Heh heh.' Easing his enormous bulk out of his chair, Max waddled off to another room.

Jack sipped his glass of wine and blinked drowsily. 'What's Max doing? I didn't quite catch what he said.'

'No one ever does.' Joanne waved a reassuring hand. 'But you get used to it after a while.' She nodded sleepily and lifted her eyes to look at Jack. 'What happened in Pittsburgh?'

'Nothing really. It was a bit of a washout,' he grunted ruefully.

'Was she nice?' The crooked red veins spreading from the corner of her eyes informed him that Joanne, whilst doing her damnedest to maintain courteous interest in his reason for being there, was totally whacked.

'Let's just say absence makes the heart grow fonder.'

In the dream, Jack's grandmother was dying. He knew it was a dream because he had already cried himself awake once, and remembered that she was already dead. But somehow he found a way back into the dream.

She was sitting in her old room, the one next to Jack's, in his parents' house in Pimlico. Her hands were red and blue, wizened with age but they did not shake. Flesh hung in crumpled folds over the corners of her mouth so that even her most radiant smile betrayed her inner sadness.

'I long for death, you see.' Her small, shrunken head shook, acknowledging the absurdity of it all. 'Mrs Emery died yesterday. You remember her, don't you Jack?'

'Yes, her son Julian is in my class at school.'

'That school of yours, I don't know. Did you read the local paper? The lowest percentage of 'O' level students in London. And you, with your intelligence.'

'I'd rather concentrate on being a good drummer than on some poxy exam.'

'Pah!' Granny's knobbly, brown walking-stick whipped through the air and the enlarged rubber tip waggled threateningly in front of Jack's nose. 'What are you going to do about getting a proper job? Eh? It's all very well when you're young but when you get to my age . . .' She lowered the cane. 'I couldn't manage without my pension, you know. What will you do?' Her tone was no longer critical, merely concerned.

'Being a musician is just like doing any other job, Granny. Sure there are bigger risks involved than being an accountant or something, but the rewards are bigger too. You can earn enough money from one hit record to retire for good.'

'Fiddlesticks,' Granny giggled at her grandson's outlandish claims.

But it was true. Admittedly, the record concerned would have to be a world wide, top ten smash, but still, the principle was there. 'What would you say to one hundred thousand pounds?'

'Thank you very much, can I keep it?' she giggled again.

'Well that's what one person can earn from one record.'

'Is it?' She shook her head disbelievingly. 'Is it really?'

'Yes.'

Staring out of the window, her steely, grey gaze grew cloudy and dull. 'Yes, you see, this isn't my world any more. The things you people get up to nowadays are too much . . . too much for this old lady to cope with. And yet, you see, I'm still here, still hanging on while young people all over the place are . . . Why only last week Mrs Emery died. She had a dog. Walked it every day. What will happen to the dog now?'

A small tear hung precariously on the edge of Jack's lower lid. He tilted his head back and sniffed, that was enough sentimentality for one day.

From downstairs, Joey's whoops of celebration howled like a police siren and the house vibrated as he thundered around, presumably playing with whatever presents he'd received. At least that would keep him occupied until the dinner guests arrived at midday. He wasn't a bad kid but Jack wasn't really in the mood for giving drumming lessons to an impatient four-year-old.

It was ten thirty according to the alarm clock in his room, and Jack stood by the open window, breathing deeply. It was a cold, cloudy day and the air tasted much fresher than it did in London. Looking out into the spacious back yard, he noticed the empty swimming pool and wished it were summer.

'What would you like for breakfasht, Jack? Flap jacksh and shyrup or French toasht and jelly. Or both?'

'I'm okay, food wise. You see, I don't usually eat breakfast and as we're having lunch –'

'You shee?' Joanne's cheeks bloated. 'You shee how eashy it ish to shay "no"?'

'Hmph hmpf,' Max coughed happily and spooned another pancake into his already bulging mouth.

'I think I'll go for a walk before lunch.'

They all stopped eating and stared up at him.

'A walk?' asked Joanne. 'Where?'

'Well, er . . . just . . . around here.' Jack waved his arms vaguely, having no particular destination in mind.

'Oh.' They went back to their meal.

Setting himself the task of walking to the end of the avenue, Jack had come to a dead end in front of a small, steep hill. Patches of grass and shrubs had made the climb easy and he sat like the king of the castle, watching over his domain. As far as the eye could see, long brown boxes alternated with small white cubes in never-ending strips of tastefully designed Lego. And yet, in every one of those identical cubicles, something different was happening. 'There's Mrs Brown, she wears a frown, and spends her Christmas all alone, and Mr Jones he moans and moans, a never-ending monotone. One more Unpleasant Valley Sunday, Here in plastic Legoland,' Jack hummed contentedly as the sun peeked out from behind a cloud.

'And you know what? He got up this. "I'm going for".'

'For a what?'

'A walk.'

'Where?'

'I don't know. Round the block. I don't know.' Max bobbed and weaved and bourbon splashed out of his glass onto the hall carpet.

Joanne's family was so large that both the living and the kitchen-cum-dining rooms were jam packed. Max and his friend had spilled out into the hall and, unbeknown to them, Jack sat above them at the top of the stairs.

'What's he like?'

'It's hard. The boy's obviously. But I don't think.'

Screwing up his face in concentration, Jack struggled to pick out the fading syllables.

'I bet the ladies. Heh heh.'

'Like uncle like nephew, uh? Ha haa!' The friend clapped Max on the back and bourbon splashed from both their glasses onto the carpet.

'What me? Nooo.'

'Are you kidding?' the friend crowed. 'What about the redhead in reception. Come onnnn. She's only been with us a week. I haven't seen you work that fast since Betty Boop. Remember her? All tits and no ass. It's a wonder she didn't fall flat on her face, ha haaa.'

Max's bobbing and weaving had reached almost epic proportions and he danced around the other man like a giant pregnant pixie.

'What is it with this new one, I mean apart from the obvious? Christ if it weren't for that uniform strapping 'em down she'd poke your eye out the minute she walked through the door, ha haa. No man, I – I'm serious, I really wanna know what it is with this broad.'

Swallowing the contents of his glass, Max flopped down onto the second step with his back to Jack and patted the space beside him. 'C'mere, c'mere I'll tell you something,' he slurred.

The friend just about managed to squeeze in next to him. 'Hmm.'

Max motioned for the man to lean closer. 'This broad is special. Real special. She likes.'

'You're kidding. Doesn't it hurt?'

'Yeah. That's why.' Max beamed delightedly.

One by one the guests began to leave until finally they'd all gone. Joanne looked even more bushed than the previous evening as she stacked the last of the plates into the dishwasher. Max had flaked out upstairs after one too many Jim Beams. Joey, who had found that being the centre of attention for seven non-stop hours was pretty hard work, joined him.

'Do you want a hand?' Jack offered.

'No thanks Jack, I'm just about finished. Maybe you could pour us both a drink? How's that sound?'

'Sounds good.'

The clenched fist in his chest gradually began to open as the bourbon slid down Jack's throat, leaving a warm trail behind it. His stiff, straight-backed posture relaxed and his stomach caught fire and glowed. Joanne's rather absurd party dress had already been replaced by a pair of dungarees and she wiped a greasy palm on her chest.

'That's quite a family you've got there.'

She laughed wearily. 'Yeah, I guess it sort of makes up for Max not having any folks over here. He loves them, just like they were his own flesh and blood.'

Jack felt sure that the delicious main course of curried goat and black-eyed peas, supplied ready-made by Joanne's mother, would not have escaped Max's notice. The rest of the family was like most others. They talked business and politics and car depreciation and all those other titles that feature heavily on the list of the world's most tedious topics.

'Your parents must be missing you this Christmas.'

'Oh, I don't know. I've been living away from home for six months now. I think they were glad to see the back of me,' he laughed.

'No, I doubt it. I don't think any mother is glad to see her son leave home. I know I'm not looking forward to when it's my turn. He's all I have.'

Jack tried to find an interesting spot on the wall to look at.

'Call your mom, Jack. Let her know you're okay.'

He had planned to ask Max for the fare back to New York later that evening, but now Joanne was forcing his hand. 'But the cost –'

'Cost schmost. I won't worry about it if you don't. Please, Jack. It would mean so much to her, I know.'

Outside in the hall, Jack began to dial. 'Hello, operator.'

'No,' Joanne's voice echoed from the kitchen. 'Dial direct, 01–01, it's cheaper.'

Jack hung up and dialled again.

Eleven

"Ow much longer you gonna be then?' Fag Ash Lil rapped her bony knuckles on the glass impatiently. Her hair was straw yellow with nicotine stains and her tongue flapped around toothless gums. She didn't really want to use the phone, having no family or friends to call, it was just her way of starting a conversation.

"Alf a mo', Grace. Look Lil, there's anuvver phone box just down the road why don't you try down there?'

'And where would that be?' she huffed defiantly.

'Just down the road,' Andy said and pointed towards Fulham Cross.

She pulled a face like a lost little girl. 'So you don't want to talk to me then?'

'Lil,' he chuckled, you had to laugh, 'I'm on the blower right now. Gissa couple a' minutes, I won't be long, all right?' Without waiting for an answer, Andy pulled the door to and resumed his conversation.

'So anyway, what presents did you get?' Grace inquired eagerly.

'The usual. After shave, socks, money.' He hadn't got past the bumfluff stage and he wouldn't be caught dead wearing tartan but one out of three wasn't bad. "Ow about you?'

'Actually, I didn't get anything from my parents this year.' There was muffled laughter, evidently Grace had company at her end of the line. 'Oh, Andy, you'll never guess what they've given me.' She paused and, for some reason, he felt reluctant to join in the game.

'A car,' he ventured lackadaisically.

'Oh my God!' Grace gasped, 'How did you know that? Andy, you're psychic.'

On my life, a fuckin' motor. Just like that. Hello Mummykins, hello Daddykins. What's that rather large parcel underneath the Christmas tree? 'I didn't know you could drive.'

'I'd almost forgotten myself. Dad taught me ages ago. He always said it would come in handy one day. I passed my test the first time but I never got around to having a car of my own.'

Andy could feel her break into one of those dazzlingly brilliant beams of delight.

'Isn't it wonderful?'

Of course it was, why did she need him to confirm it for her. 'Yeah, great.'

'I'll be driving back in it. It's a Mini, second-hand of course, but it's in really good condition. Fifteen hundred pounds,' she whispered solemnly. 'It's black with tinted windows, Dad thought that might appeal to me. What are you doing on New Year's Eve? Perhaps we could go out for the day. The seaside perhaps.'

'Yeah, great.'

The corner of Lil's battered, black handbag caught his eye. Something rusty brown stuck out of it and Andy recognised the colour immediately. It was a tenner, one of how many? Lil may have had a few screws loose but her flat, on the top floor of Clem Attlee House, was a mini-fortress. Everybody knew she had money but no one had ever managed to get past the barrage of bolts. It had never occurred to Andy that she would be stupid enough to carry it around.

'That's ever such a nice haircut, Andrew, who did that for you?'

'Mr Gliszczynski.' Most of his customers called him Mr Gee but Andy never had any problem with the pronunciation.

'Maybe I ought to have one like that.' Lil's brittle hair crackled as she ran her arthritic fingers through it.

'Yeah, I reckon you should,' Andy agreed. Somewhere beneath the ingrained layers of dirt and grime, there was a handsome woman. Knock off forty years and he probably wouldn't have kicked her out of bed himself. But now she was just a batty old hag whose empty existence made a mockery of the money she hoarded. In her hands, the cash was worthless. She didn't even drink.

'My Albert said to me the other day, he said, Marion –' Her husband was the only person who had called her by that name and he'd been dead for years. '– in all the years that we've been married, I've never so much as looked at another woman.'

''E must a' spent a lot a' time bumpin' into fings,' Andy quipped.

'I can't understand why, I said, I'm as plain as a pikestaff, I've not done anything with my hair for days –' Decades. '– but Albert says, I'm not interested in fancy hair dos an' that, when I look at you I see a princess –'

''E was a copper, wernee?' Andy asked, eager to change the subject.

'Twenty-two years of loyal service to the force,' she affirmed proudly, 'never a day off sick.'

'What, not even when 'e 'ad 'is operation?'

'What operation?'

Andy sat in Bishop's Park with the collar of his Crombie coat turned up around his ears. A freezing wind chilled him to the bone but he stayed quite still. He was an idiot, an utter wally. There were so many so-called 'bad' things he'd done in his life, why was mugging Lil so different? It wasn't just Lil, there had been other times when Andy found himself incapable of capitalising on a situation. He had a soft streak, there was no denying it. A uselessly vulnerable and tender part that he wished had been removed along with his tonsils. Carl had no more brains than he; what made him the leader of the crew was his total lack of emotion. Carl would have had Lil for breakfast; if she resisted he probably would have killed her.

An aeroplane roared overhead, its wing lights flashing red and green in the murky, purple sky as the setting sun strained through a sea of clouds. And there was Jack at the other end of the scale, soft as shit, hanging round with a load of wimps, but having the time of his life. If Jack had taken Grace home to his parents they wouldn't've batted a bloody eyelid. And if Carl had shagged her, a doubtful premise at best, he probably would have beaten her up and robbed her, without being foolish enough to think that there was any future in the relationship.

Andy gazed around to see if there were any other poor wretches who had nothing better to do than hang around a huge heap of horse-shit. Captain Spastic lurched into view and began negotiating the home stretch. Dressed in flimsy black running shorts and a white vest, he moaned with exertion and veered involuntarily to the right. His elbow jerked out to one side and his arm flew over his head in a crazy, flapping motion. 'Geeeeuggggh!' With extraordinary effort, he forced his twisting, uncoordinated legs to carry him forward once more. Sweat poured from his forehead as he approached Andy in agonised slow motion. No matter what the weather or time of year, Captain Spastic lapped the park once a day. Though Andy was not always present, he knew it to be true and couldn't help being impressed. It was obviously an attempt at rehabilitating his deformed, disobedient body.

'Merry Christmas, mate,' he said as the Captain honked like a wounded seal and pounded past.

Wandering into the living room, Andy was greeted by Her Majesty Queen Elizabeth the Second sounding off about how much nicer people ought to be to each other. The old man was a stickler for respect where royalty was concerned. Andy kept schtum until the flaccid monologue finally came to an end.

'You cop for that, did ya?' the old man challenged.

'Yeah, yeah,' Andy and Colin sighed in unison and grinned at each other conspiratorially.

The old man guzzled at the bottle of Glenfiddich and wiped the pale yellow dribbles from his scratchy chin.

'Gi's a slug,' Andy requested and the old man slapped the bottle into his hand with no argument. Colin's eyes filled with dull aggression as he witnessed this silent sign of comradeship. Swigging the smooth spirit, Andy wondered whether to pass the bottle to his brother and then thought better of it, either the old man would object or Colin would feel patronised or both. Anyway, if he wanted it, he could always ask.

The standardly bland Thames Television announcer informed his viewers that *Thunderball* was about to be repeated for the umpteenth time. Hurrying off to the kitchen, Colin returned with his tin of Quality Street and sat with his eyes glued to the commercials as though the film had already commenced.

'Jesus Christ, it bored the fuckin' pants off me the first time I saw it. How many more times?'

'Ian Fleming,' said the old man, pointing at the screen as the familiar guitar based theme clanked along busily, punctuated by blasting horns.

'Nah. 'S George Lazenby you're finkin' of,' Colin announced proudly, 'and it's a different film. You're finkin' of the one where they go skiing but that one's called *On 'Er M–*'.

'Shut it,' the old man drawled with bored annoyance. 'Ian Fleming,' he repeated, 'was the man 'oo wrote all the James Bond books. They will keep turnin' 'em into films but they're nuffin' like the books.'

''Ow come?' asked Andy, interested to know what was the difference between the two.

'Search me, son, but the books are ten times better.'

That wouldn't be difficult. 'When did you read 'em?' Andy couldn't remember ever having seen the old man with a book in his hand. Whoops, tell a lie, there was that brief flirtation with the 'Confessions of a . . .' series. Each book consisted of a few slices of soft smut sprinkled in amongst a hundred and fifty pages of superfluous waffle. The juicy bits were signposted as the relevant pages had their corners folded over and Andy remembered jerking off whilst reading them before he had spunk to shoot. The memory of those dry runs seemed peculiarly precious.

'Fuck me, I can't remember,' the old man snapped, pissed off at his own forgetfulness rather than Andy's innocuous inquiry. 'Years ago.'

Before Mum left us? Andy wanted to ask but didn't.

'Yeah I used to read a lot in them days.'

'What else?'

Wading through decades of seventy per cent proof fog, the old man's concentration was visible, almost audible. His mouth moved to speak several times as clumps of information presented themselves in his mind like mis-matched jigsaw pieces. Andy's own mind back-tracked wildly, desperately trying to find a name to jog the old man's memory. William Shakespeare. And? Think, first names. Andrew . . . no. Patrick . . . no. Mary . . . Mary . . . there was a writer called Mary and it had something to do with films but . . . shit. William Shakespeare. Andy had that name carved into his cerebral organ like a tattoo.

Twelve

The presents were beautifully wrapped, naturellement. The wrapping paper on each had a different design and neither of them had anything to do with Christmas. The framed original silk-screen print of silver birch trees had been hard to find; Nat loved the artist's work. 'Test Match', a board game of skill, speed and cricketing knowledge had caught Chrissy's eye, collecting dust on the top shelf of her local newsagent a few weeks ago, and Ben, for some obscure reason, was an avid fan of the West Indies first eleven. The silk-screen print was a sensible purchase, she supposed, since the artist was gaining rapidly in stature and Nat was building a modest collection, but the board game was a typical example of her ostentatious frivolity when choosing presents for others. 'Look what an amazing amount of thought I put into this, aren't I clever?' 'Test Match' would end up collecting dust on a different shelf, that was all.

The gifts she expected to receive in return would be much more down to earth: a bottle of exotic booze, Sambuca perhaps, and a box of chocolates. Perfect presents designed to indulge her in luxury she would not normally lavish on herself. There was no attempt at inventiveness, just an awareness and acceptance of what the receiver really wants. And that, in an analogous nutshell, was why Nat and Ben had a solid marriage and a loving son while Chrissy had . . . what? Artifice. A career promoting other people's talent and a group of acquaintances, not large enough or dear enough to be called a circle of friends. Undirected anger ached in her throat and she coughed, wanting to cry or puke or something, anything that would expel the destructive negativity forcing her hands to contract in fists and her toes to curl downwards and dig into the soles of her shoes. Staring hard at the neat packages on the kitchen table, she tried to disintegrate them. It didn't work. Reluctantly, Chrissy scooped the presents off the table and slid them into a chunky plastic bag.

It wasn't the money, she could well afford to travel everywhere by cab. No, it was the hollow fascination of being forced to sit face to face with somebody. Strangers on a train. And when the opposite seat was vacant, she stared at her reflection, clear, against the seemingly static grey blackness of the tunnel wall. A youngish woman who looked pale and drawn, not excessively so, but whose impish features would have been so much more suited to a brash, saucy smirk. Instead she looked like a derelict Bisto Kid. Some people might think she was a little under-developed, physically speaking, through no fault of her own. At least God had played fair, she had brains to compensate. Now that comment about her being young*ish* was an interesting one, a matter of opinion, you might say. After all, is the glass half full or half empty? Three score years and ten.

The walk to her sister's was quite a complex one. Chrissy used to get lost on the way. After crossing Victoria Street into Pimlico, the back streets twisted and turned making it difficult to keep her bearings. At last the dingy little basement flat came into view and she descended the wrought iron spiral staircase. She still couldn't understand why, after being successfully burgled five times, Nat and Ben had kept it on. Not only that, but they insisted on renting rather than buying which was the same as throwing their money down the toilet in Chrissy's opinion.

Rapping her knuckles on the door pane, she shifted from one foot to the other and breathed visibly into the cold night air. Otto. There it was again. That one single word just kept popping into her head.

The sound of running feet thundered up to the other side of the door, the lock clicked open and the thunder rolled away again. This was Nat's way of saying 'Hi, how are you? Excuse me a moment while I check on the supper.'

As she walked along the hall towards the kitchen, Chrissy noticed the familiar smell. It was damp and probably had something to do with the flat being below street level. All at once her nostrils developed a maddening tickle and she sneezed several times.

'Gesundheit,' Nat and Ben shouted simultaneously.

Libby had obviously decided to grace them with his presence and, sure enough, there he sat on the dining table with one paw held limp in mid air. Liberace, probably the world's only proven homosexual tom.

'He still gets up your nose, doesn't he?' Nat said as she removed a deliciously crispy looking cheese and aubergine flan from the oven.

As well as her nostrils, Chrissy's eyes began to itch and she rubbed the corners gently. Continuing his impersonation of a teapot, Libby regarded her with mock innocence.

'We've both had a bloody awful day and we're already pissed,' Ben announced grandly. 'I haven't had this much fun since the cat died.' Libby's paw dropped abruptly. 'Whoops, sorry. We've still got that day to look forward to, haven't we?' Unable to stand any further abuse, Libby leapt down onto the lino and stalked out of the room, swishing his tail in distaste. 'Cocky little poof. We probably won't see him for days. Anyway, come on, Chris. Cheer us up, tell us a joke.' Ben offered her a glass of red wine which she gulped down, anxious not to be left at the starting post.

At midnight Ben proposed his umpteenth toast. 'To the abolition of Chrishmush, Eanshter and all the other God related sh–'

The phone rang, cutting off his less than eloquent speech. Nat went to answer it. 'Hello? Oh Jack, how lovely to hear from you. Great timing. What? I said great timing. A minute later and it would have been Boxing Day. What? Oh yes of course, I forgot about the time difference. What have you been doing?' Nat's side of the conversation degenerated into enthusiastic umms and ahhs.

'Ben, are you falling asleep?' asked Chrissy as her brother-in-law began to nod off.

'My shun. Sssson,' he corrected himself. 'My ssson, the musssician.'

'Ben, quickly,' Nat shouted. 'Jack needs an address in New York. What about that Ableberg woman, does she still have an apartment there?'

Ben got up and lurched into the hall passing Nat on her way in.

'What Ableberg woman?' asked Chrissy, intrigued.

'Ableberg, Ablestein, what do I know? Something like that.' If Nat disliked a person intensely, she would pretend to forget their name.

'Jewish, by any chance?'

'How would I know? I've really no idea.'

Ooh, touchy. A different approach, perhaps. 'I mean, are you sure about her. Jack is at a very impressionable –'

'Now hold on a minute. Just because she let Ben get his feet under the table you don't think –' Nat stopped abruptly and gave Chrissy a sly, sideways glance. 'Very clever. Ten out of ten.' Her face relaxed into a knowing smile.

'Before you were married?'

'Yes, of course.'

Stupid question, really.

'He was writing short stories for a science-fiction magazine, an American publication. The pay was good, for those days, so we thought we'd blow some on a trip to New York. Ben wanted to visit the magazine's headquarters and I'd always wanted to see New York but –'

'You didn't make it.' It was all coming back now. As soon as she found out about the trip, Phyllis had developed a strange illness. Whilst having no obvious symptoms, it was horrifically painful and required that she be attended to, at all times, by a responsible adult. Being ten years younger than her then twenty-two-year old sister, Chrissy hadn't exactly fitted the bill. And apart from Nat, there was no one else. They both fell silent and Ben's voice became audible.

'*East* Second Street. Remember that. Nearly all the streets have an east and a west. You don't want West Second Street, what do you want?' He paused. 'That's right. And the girl's name is?

Correct. Now get off the line before Max has to sell his house to pay for this call.' He certainly seemed to have sobered up. 'Yeah. Yeah, you too.' There was another brief pause. 'Max! What's happening?' Ben closed the kitchen door and his voice became indistinct.

'Well?' asked Chrissy avidly. 'How's Mr Kerouac?'

'Apparently,' Nat began, 'Pittsburgh was very boring and Philadelphia's just like any other suburb, so he's leaving for New York tomorrow.'

'And the girl?'

'I think it fell through. You know Jack.' They both laughed. 'How are things with you, Chris?'

'I think I might be onto something.' It must have been the booze. This was far too dangerous a game to be playing with Nat, they knew each other too well.

'But there's a problem, isn't there?'

Drat. She had better not give any more away.

'A big problem,' Nat emphasised the word 'big' in a slow drawl and checked Chrissy's eyes for confirmation.

If she lied now, Nat's curiosity would only deepen. She might even put two and two together. 'He's a lot younger than I am.' That was good, keep it vague.

'And perhaps there are mutual acquaintances who might not approve? Getting warm?'

'Okay, Sherlock, enough already.' Chrissy's heart began to pound.

Inching slowly towards each other, Nat's eyebrows met above the bridge of her nose. 'Me? You think I won't approve? Who is it? Tell me. Whoever it is, I promise I'll be pleased.'

'About what?' Leaning against the door frame, Ben rubbed his temples vigorously.

'Chris has got some surprise celebrity lined up for an interview,' Nat responded, quick as a flash. 'It's supposed to be a secret.' Test Match commentary represented the bulk of Ben's radio listening and well Nat knew it.

'Oh,' said Ben, not bothering to pretend interest.

'Let me guess,' she continued. 'Is it a group or singer?'

'Group.'

'All male?'

'Nope.'

'Ah well, that narrows it down quite a lot. This group, they wouldn't originate from Sweden, by any chance?'

Grace was with her family in Peterborough and Jack was in Philadelphia with his. But poor Otto had to make do with Christmas alone. Wouldn't it be a shame if someone didn't drop in and say 'hello'?

'Mm?'

Again, that strange way of moving his entire head instead of just the eyes.

'Oh, Chrissy. I – uh –' Otto held the door open but did not invite her in.

He had company. Female, she could smell it. 'If it's inconvenient?'

Looking puzzled, he offered a weak smile. 'Do you want to come in?' He stood aside.

Hardly the most gracious of welcomes but under the circs. Now she really could smell it. Subtle, expensive perfume. A class act.

Otto led the way, trundling unsteadily along the hall and into the living room. All the side lamps were off and the main spotlights had been dimmed to a vague sepia. The dimmer switch buzzed frantically, as though under great stress. Three young girls sat in a huddle at the far end of the dining table. They each had golden brown skin and thick, black wavy hair. The middle girl wore a large Homburg and a gold watch chain dangled from her brocade waistcoat pocket. She looked first at Chrissy, then at Otto, and jerked her head in curt approval.

'Is very good shit today,' she said, taking off her hat. It left a deep dent in her hair but she shook her head once and it was gone.

Chrissy hadn't done anything with her own, absurdly fine and straggly hair, for ages.

Running her finger around the hat band, the girl fished out a tiny packet. Carefully, she undid the packet and tapped a small quantity of brown powder onto a round face mirror. 'I leave my works at home. It's not safe in the streets, you know? You got a note so we can snort this?'

'Sorry.' Otto shrugged.

'Hey, forget sorry, how you gonna pay?'

'I'll get it as soon as the banks are open. Honest. You wouldn't take a cheque?'

The girl stared at him and sighed. 'Look if it was just me, okay. But I gotta look after my sisters, you know? It's business.'

The other two seemed to have only a vague idea of what was happening. Perhaps they couldn't speak English.

'But you've already laid some out. Come on Lila, please?'

'How much is it?' Chrissy blurted, before she had a chance to change her mind.

'Are you sure?' Otto asked meekly.

Lila smiled. Another customer. 'What we have here,' she said in an unnecessarily slow, instructive voice and indicated the already open packet, 'is a ten pound bag.'

Scooping out her purse from her handbag, Chrissy passed a ten pound note to Lila. After holding it up to what little light there was, she seemed satisfied with its authenticity and rolled the note into a tube. Putting one end of the tube to her nostril, she placed a finger over the other nostril, bent forward and sniffed some of the powder. She passed the tube to one of her sisters who did the same.

'And what's your contribution? You just sit here and sniff it, do you?' Chrissy mocked as the third sister got stuck in.

'N-no, Lila's okay,' Otto stammered and a genuine look of concern spread across his face.

Lila came from Portugal. She talked about her oppressive, religious upbringing and described at length the obsessive need to get away. On landing in England aged seventeen, she had quickly sussed out that there was no work available. At least, not the kind she wanted. Hence the dope dealing. It wasn't such a bad life. There was always a chance of being busted but dealing in small quantities kept the risk of a prison sentence down to the minimum. After setting up the business, she went back to Portugal and returned with her two sisters, also eager to get out from under. Otto was one of a number of off-and-on clients. Lila didn't have no time for junkies. No, she couldn't reveal her source and Chrissy felt silly for asking such a naive question.

Thelonious Monk honked and jerked his way through a solo piano piece.

'You never asked me why I came,' Chrissy observed quietly.

The eerie harmonics and child-like invention of the pianist seemed to suit her current situation down to the ground. It was two o'clock on Boxing Day morning and it felt like it. She had no desire to go home but she was tired.

Rustling around on his beanbag, Otto turned to face her. His pupils had contracted to the size of pinheads giving his emerald eyes a sort of Paul Newman intensity. 'I think you want to make love to me.'

Of all the phrases he could have picked to describe it, that was the perfect choice. Now all she had to do was say yes.

'I'm not sure. I mean, I think I do. It's so difficult to explain, you see . . . when you say . . .' She lowered her voice in an attempt to impersonate him. "I think you want to make love to me," I know there's more to it than that. For me. What I'm trying to say is – I know I'm not putting this very well . . .'

Shaking his head in disagreement, Otto gave her an encouraging glance. 'We could just . . . sleep together.'

Somehow he managed to make it sound even more exciting than making love.

A barely audible drum roll grew louder and louder and suddenly exploded into crashing cymbals, signalling the start of the next tune. A seemingly ordinary piano scale became curious and questioning as each melodic line ended in an odd, unexpected discord. Everything in the garden is rosy, except that the roses aren't red, they're blue.

'He's really very good, isn't he?' said Chrissy.

'Monk? He's a genius. There's no other word. He helps you see things from a different perceptive.' Perspective? 'Like doing drugs. He lets you know there's no right way or wrong way, just different ways.'

The stereo speakers were placed in diagonally opposite corners, filling the whole room with a rich, resonant sound.

'Would you like to try some of this?' asked Otto as he tapped some more heroin onto the mirror. 'After all, it is yours.'

No. In one of Jack's few demonstrations of restraint, he had said that this was one drug he would never touch. And what was good enough for Jack . . .

'Do you have any. . . ?' The appropriate word momentarily escaped her.

'Smoke? No, sorry. Jack usually organises that, I don't really know the dealer that well. I could try –'

'No, don't bother. It was just a thought.' Smiling ruefully, Chrissy felt another wave of exhaustion wash over her.

'It might help you sleep,' Otto offered as he ripped a corner out of the front page of *Cosmopolitan* and rolled it into a tube.

A warm, cosy feeling enveloped Chrissy like a womb. She was safe. Nausea lapped at her like an over-affectionate dog and her forehead began to itch. She scratched at it roughly and the itch hopped, like a flea, to the end of her nose. Rubbing her nose between her thumb and forefinger, Chrissy felt the irritation move again, this time to her chin. After a few minutes she gave up trying to catch it.

'– who says that she thinks my show is obscene. What a ridiculous suggestion. Oh and by the way, have you heard the one about the gay milkman? He never leaves an empty behind – all right, I admit it – the show is the teensiest bit smutty but you wouldn't have it any other way would you? You would? Oh well be like that then.' A totally anonymous disc faded up underneath the deejay's prattling. 'It's five minutes to nine this Boxing Day morning, here on LWS. If you've just begun to recover from that hangover, why bother? You'll only have to do it all over again in five days time.' Newton was right. Gravity really did exist. Every inch of Chrissy's body was being drawn towards the floor by an invisible magnet. Otto was still asleep, thank the Lord. Switching off the radio alarm, Chrissy attempted to rise from her sitting position at the edge of the bed.

One side of the King's Road was solid with traffic heading for Sloane Square. Luckily, it wasn't the side Otto was driving on. He had appeared in the kitchen, while Chrissy was making herself a coffee, and offered to take her home.

In spite or perhaps because of the fact that she didn't drive, Chrissy had become very aware of the way other people handled a car. Otto's way was smooth and relaxed, almost effortless. The Citroën's suspension made the ride seem more like they were in a hovercraft than a car.

Even today, handfuls of punks continued their endless pilgrimage up and down the King's Road, eager to confirm that this was truly a sacred place. Boy looked a mite more welcoming without the obligatory bored-looking shop assistant snarling with contempt at the customers. It was amazing anyone had the nerve to go in there. Jack, of course, had an account paid for by the band's record company and regaled Chrissy with stories of how both Rod Stewart and Warren Beatty had been refused entry on the grounds that they were too old. According to Jack, the staff seemed to spend half their time selling Sex Pistols bootlegs. Opposite Boy, the Chelsea Odeon announced a late night showing of *American Graffiti*. On the last Saturday of each month, Capital, the rival radio station, aired their fifties rock 'n' roll show, 'Cruisin'', inviting people to drag up and down the King's Road in their customised cars, and the Odeon responded with yet another re-run. Chrissy loved to stand and watch the low, low riders and old Fords with their backs jacked right up, the drivers with their gigantic quiffs and their girlfriends in skirts so bulky they dare not get out of the car for fear of not being able to get back in.

'This one?' Otto flicked on the indicator.

'Yes.'

Swinging left off the New King's Road, he parked the car. They walked the few steps to Chrissy's front door and stood on the porch. 'Come in.' She made a move to unlock the door.

'No, I'd better get back.' He leaned forward to kiss her. His tongue squirmed against her clenched teeth and he pulled away quickly. 'Will I see you again?' He looked hurt.

She remembered how they had kissed just a few hours ago, lying naked and warm in each other's arms. But they didn't make love. 'Are you sure you want to?'

'There's a party on New Year's Eve. I could pick you up here at about eight thirty.'

'Okay.'

On the other side of the door Chrissy burst into a fit of hard, hollow, humourless laughter. She had to have a bath. On the inside as well as the outside.

The navy skirt, the plain orange blouse and the rainbow coloured Marks & Spencer knickers were thrown into the wicker laundry basket in the bathroom. She flipped the water heater control to maximum. 'Hail Mary, full of grace. The Lord is with thee . . .'

'Oh no, Sharon, look at my face.' For the first time in her life Chrissy wished the show would hurry up and come to an end. Even her favourite record of all time, Stevie Wonder's swinging version of 'Blowin' In The Wind', hadn't managed to lift her stupor. Although she felt tired, she didn't feel tired enough. The thought of food was peculiarly elusive though she hadn't eaten anything since the meal at Nat's the night before. The only taste her mind could get a firm grip on was chocolate. A Mars Bar or something like that.

At half past one, while Jim did his fifteen minute news feature, she went to the canteen. Dean Brando had a white pimple nestling beneath the edge of his nostril. Obviously an Invigel user. She nearly gagged on the coffee he gave her. She'd asked for it strong, but you could resurface a road with that. It did, however, prove ideal for dunking Mars Bars into and she went back to the counter and bought two more. After she'd finished the fourth, Chrissy felt sick.

'Hi Mack.' She waved the burly security guard over to her table.

'Ta luv.' He plopped into a chair and wheezed with relief. 'I'm that bloody knackered.'

He pronounced the syllable 'blood' so that it rhymed with 'hood', just as Chrissy had done years ago before she acquired the bland, standard Oxbridge accent she heard herself speaking now. The change hadn't been a conscious one, but hanging around with Julia and her circle of friends had gradually worn away the rough edges. And now all that remained was an inability to pronounce 'castle' as though it rhymed with 'parcel'. It never did and never would.

'I've been on t' go since half past two this morning.'

Roughly the time that Chrissy and Otto had gone to bed.

'Do you know,' Mack continued, evidently about to tell her something that she didn't, 'I've been on t' phone best part of t' night. First there were practical jokers, then there were t' police –'

'What happened?'

'Nowt really. Some silly bugger cracked on there were a bomb in t' building.'

Oh, was that all.

Thirteen

'Most of you may remember this summer as being remarkable for two things – the Queen's silver jubilee and the Sex Pistols' shocking success with a single decrying the whole affair. Meanwhile something far more interesting was happening. A small independent record label decided to re-release a classic song recorded the year before.' 'One two three four five six,' an awkward, adenoidal monotone counted the song in. 'If this is the New Wave,' Chrissy purred sexily, 'then I'm all for it.'

Andy had never thought of her voice as being sexy before, but he certainly heard it now. A faint, sleepy hiss accompanied her usual light, expressive modulations. With this added dimension she could make the telephone directory sound like hard core pornography. Andy listened to the record. What the fuckinell was all that about, ay? The man droned on, horrendously limp and out of tune, as though purposely trying to turn in the worst vocal performance possible. His diction descended into a series of autistic moans with only the words 'roadrunner' and 'radio on' remaining discernible. And there was Chrissy telling everybody it was great. The musicianship was so unbelievably amateur, anybody could do it. Andy kicked himself mentally for not having taken Jack more seriously when he announced he was going to form a group. He wondered whether the bird in The Destroyers was any good. The brain-damaged meanderings he was being subjected to at the moment were ample proof that you didn't need to be. Perhaps Jack would have time for two groups, The Destroyers and. . . ? Andy tried to think of a good name for a group. Well that would depend on what kind of music they played and, since it was his band, he decided it would be ska, the original skinhead sound. Something you could really grind to, a big brassy jerking off-beat with flaring tam-tam rolls courtesy of Jack 'Sly' Shaw and a hard urgent lyric about ghetto life in the concrete jungle or a slick slab of sex delivered on bended knees by Andy 'The Man' Mason. A name with the word ska in it, like The Skatalites? Nah, too obvious.

'A record of truly universal appeal, that was Roadrunner by Jonathan Richman and the Modern Lovers,' Chrissy informed her listener deliberately. 'After the break, what say we take a little Walk On The Wild Side? It's twelve thirty this Boxing Day afternoon on LWS and here's Jim Ellington with the news headlines.'

The Universals. Switching the radio off, Andy propped himself up in bed, re-ran his pool table fantasy and masturbated. The image of Grace slipped through his mind like water through a sieve and he laboured to hold it in place. But her features were becoming less and less distinct until he was left with an overgrown foetus, totally lacking in any character. 'It might as well be anyone.' Her hair was in beaded plaits and her jeans were around her ankles but everything in between was an amorphous brown stain. Even the colour was wrong and Andy switched nervously to his old and faithful fantasy. He and his step-sister, Sue, pressed passionately against each other in a nude embrace, in his mind she was still only eleven years old. They were fucking without actually doing so and the sensation was like eating Cornish ice cream on a balmy autumn evening. Not vanilla. Cornish. The room was fairly non-descript except for the sofa that they sat on, a two-seater with warm, orangey red rose patterns covering its firm but yielding shape. The removal men had come to collect it a month after his mother walked out and it was the first time it had occurred to him that she wouldn't be coming back. Sue's thoughts melted, telepathically, into his own like a pair of hands with gradually interlocking fingers. They both knew that, just outside the room, the old man, the old dear and Colin were waiting in anticipation for them to come out and announce their engagement. The air was full of good thoughts and benevolence, a cushion of slow motion. If, in this wonderland, they should fall to the floor, it would turn to rubber and bounce them back up again like a trampoline. Susy smiled, sensing that the time was right and Andy stopped sliding his foreskin back and forth, savouring the moments that he knew would soon be over, at least until the next time.

Colin was already up, as expected, looking as bright eyed and bushy tailed as it was possible for him to be. The old man probably wouldn't surface until around two o'clock and, as Andy couldn't face an attempt at conversation first thing in the morning, he snapped the TV on and cracked one of the two Brews he had left. Collapsing into the old man's armchair, he took a mega-swig and demolished three-quarters of the can in one go.

'Better not still be there when 'e wakes up, 'e'll 'ave you, you know.'

Sometimes the old man could get bolshy about Andy sitting in his chair while Colin simply never dared, not through fear but a misguided sense of loyalty to his father which, in turn, triggered a perverse allegiance to Colin in Andy. He was reminded of Harry H. Corbett in *Steptoe and Son* except that, in Andy's case, the problems were more complex. If it were just him and the old man, he would have left home the day he was expelled from school. 'What else is on?' he asked.

Colin rustled the *Sun* noisily as he searched for the middle pages. With his back to his brother, Andy heard him swallow hard, the usual reaction to his daily dose of tit on page three.

'Come on,' he cajoled impatiently as Colin's breathing increased in volume and depth, 'you've been gawpin' at 'er for the last two days.' Some brainless bint wearing a G-string and a gormless grin, not forgetting the obligatory arched back pose as though she were sitting on a block of ice in the middle of the Antarctic.

Colin hummed with fake casualness and eventually turned his way to the TV section.

'Uh-uh *Arise . . . My Love*,' he struggled.

Christ it was only three words. "Oo's in it?' It had to be better than this dodgy old war movie.

'Uh . . . Ray Mill and . . . uh . . . Cl-Claude . . .'

'Ray 'oo? Never 'eard of 'im. 'Ere gissat a mo',' Andy turned and held out his hand.

"Old on,' Colin whined defensively and hunched over the newspaper possessively, 'I 'ad it first.'

Andy sighed and decided to find out what else was on for himself. A bunch of poofs in smocks delivered their drones of praise to the Lord, the cast of *The Good Life* continued to be incredibly nice and there was that dodgy old war movie again. 'You stupid berk, it's Ray Milland,' he laughed, recognising the Man With The X-Ray Eyes. Now there was a movie he had seen countless times and would gladly sit through again, but unfortunately he wasn't being given the chance.

'Uh . . . Claude – I fink they must've spelt it wrong, Claude somebody.'

'What *are* you on about?'

'Ray Mill and Claude . . . Claude.'

Polishing off the Brew, Andy went to the fridge and got the last one. Though *Arise My Love* was not the racy bit of fluff he had been hoping for, Ray Mill and Claude Claude would simply have to do.

Tears welled up in the old man's eyes and Andy's followed suit. It wasn't the emotion with which Shirley Bassey delivered the lyrics that made him cry, though the overall effect was pretty painful, but the way the old man reacted to it. Andy wondered whether the old man fancied her. But the old man, with his whisky breath and blotchy red skin, was past the point of no return, bird-wise. He just didn't care any more.

'Fuckin' fabulous,' the old man's resonant sinuses reflected the tears in his eyes and he sniffed powerfully and swallowed. 'You cop for that, did ya?'

The two brothers grunted one after another, like a single person indicating the negative.

'Old Andy boy 'ere was gonna be a singer once,' Colin smirked, 'made any good records lately, 'ave ya?'

Andy was bursting to tell Colin of his plans for the future with The Universals but he knew better than to rise to the bait. 'Yeah, me last one went Top Ten.'

'Huh.'

'Yeah, it was called "My Bruvver's A Total Fuckin' Moron".' Colin's eyes dulled. 'Great lyrics. Wanna 'ear 'em?' And his head began to twitch.

'Your muvver,' the old man slurred.

That was enough, Andy didn't want to hear any more. There was something incredibly pathetic about him when he got like this. Repentant. He was a tough old git and his dignity was in his ability to keep going, but these occasional outbursts of maudlin despair were getting more frequent. During them, he would want to hug Colin, who was much too baffled to resist, and he regaled them both with elaborate descriptions of how wonderful his ex-wife was, what a blessing she had been to him, how he never should have left her. It was strange, but in these moods he would refuse to accept that it had been the other way around. 'Your muvver,' he repeated, unleashing a new avalanche of regretful observations about his one and only true love. The phrase 'your mother' seemed to indicate that he felt himself unworthy of her memory. Andy remembered how they had all trudged along to Kilburn Cemetery in the pouring rain.

Wearing his only suit, the old man had looked as if he had been summoned to appear in court while Colin clumped along like Frankenstein in a jacket the sleeves of which just about reached his elbows and trousers flying at half-mast above the top of his dirty grey socks. Andy's feet were wet and cold, his legs ached from the vast distance they had covered. And they never did see Mum. While they were heading towards the bone orchard, her body was being burned on the other side of the borough, in Kilburn Crematorium.

Andy's jaw hung in mute astonishment at the crumpet that made Fiona Richmond look like Julie Andrews, complete with habit. She was a cat, a leopard coiled and ready to spring an attack on any unsuspecting fool that happened to walk by. A pencil skirt hugged her twin dagger legs like black cling-film. The legs, a smooth and shapely cream, had their calf muscles pulled taut to balance against the acute angle of her high heels. She stood with her legs slightly apart in a rocksteady, gunslinger's stance, powerful, firm. Somewhere up in the sky, God had a little shed, and when he had nothing better to do, he'd go down to that shed and whittle. Away from the main conveyor belt of his standard designs, he'd pursue his hobby of creating the perfect human body. Sometimes, and rightly so, those bodies found their way into show business and became famous but other times, they'd just pop up on the corner of your street. Or in your local. Her long, thin nose glinted under the soft lights. When she smiled, it was warm and inviting and cold and threatening all at the same time. Her skinny nostrils twitched like a rabbit and her coal black eyes narrowed to laser beam intensity.

'Meet the wife,' Carl grinned, introducing his escort. 'Yvette, this is Andy.'

'Pleased to meet you.' She raised one eyebrow, lowered it and then raised the other.

Wow. The light seemed to be brighter around her than anywhere else in the pub and Andy inched into her personal spotlight. Although the hubbub of voices was loud, he heard her spittle click as she opened her mouth to speak again.

'Carl informs me that you're the best of friends.'

A rubber hammer thumped in the back of Andy's throat and he put his pint to his lips and poured it down.

The evening had been dead up until now. Earlier on Leon and Spig, the two youngest Churchill skins, had popped in for a swift jar or three. Everybody knew that they, along with Andy, were under age but Dan Spiggot Sr, Spig's old man, didn't mind and, since he ran the pub, neither did anyone else. But Leon and Spig were still kids and after the third pint they got that watery, room-spinning-round, look in their eyes and politely excused themselves before buggering off to puke. Andy was also on his third pint, the difference being that one pint of Brew equalled two pints of anything else.

'Oi, Mason, where's yer manners?' Carl had that look on his

face, somewhere between a snarl and a smile, you never knew where you were with that look.

'Watchew 'avin?' asked Andy, pulling himself together.

'Umm . . .' Yvette pondered, leaning forward over the bar to get a better butcher's at what was available. Andy felt Carl's eyes burning into him and he wished Grace was here. No he didn't. Yes he *did*.

'Sssnakebite,' Carl hissed and laughed.

'And I'll have a barley wine,' said Yvette.

'And 'ave one yourself, Dan,' Andy said as he paid for the drinks. Holding out the glass to Yvette, he caught a flash of familiar expression on her face. 'I ain't seen you about before.'

'No,' she agreed. They both turned to Carl.

'That's 'cos we only met yes'day.'

'What, on the march?' Andy could hardly believe his ears. The National Front had taken exception to the Paki shops staying open over Christmas – it was another example of how they were bleeding the nation dry. A demonstration had been organised to take place in the East End of London, which happened to be miles away, so Andy had declined Carl's offer to join him. 'Wha' 'appened?' It hadn't been on the news or anything like that.

'We won,' Yvette beamed triumphantly.

'There was a scrap?' he asked earnestly.

'Nah,' Carl informed him reluctantly.

'But we won,' Yvette repeated proudly, 'not one shop stayed open for business.'

'That's ace, really fuckin' ace,' Andy found himself saying, 'what's next on the agenda, Brenda?'

'Pardon?'

''Ee means are there any other demos lined up?' Carl translated.

'Well . . . let me think.'

'So you're a Front member, are ya? Official, like?'

'Yep, and she's gonna fix me up an' all. Give a couple a' years and you'll be able to join.'

Downing his pint, Andy ordered another.

'I'll get that,' said Yvette.

'See that,' said Carl, 'how many uvver birds d'you know who'd put their 'ands in their pockets wivvout bein' asked?'

Staggering up the Fulham Road, Andy lurched into Beaufort Street. Shelley Mellors lived here. She was an old classmate from Westminster Comp. A bit on the bony side, though perhaps she'd fattened up over the two years since he'd last seen her, but she had class, almost as much as . . . The exact amount of Brews he'd consumed was blurry but Andy felt on top of it. Just. Anyway he was on his way to see Shelley because he needed a fuckin' fuck, ha ha. Maybe her old dear'd like to join in as well.

Shelley was the bird who had offered him the chance to have his evil way with her on two separate occasions and he had bottled them both. The first time, he and Jack had double dated with Shelley and Dawn who were baby-sitting at a house in Vauxhall. The two girls lay on the bed, on the fuckin' *bed* mind you, while he and Jack sat on the floor beside them and pretended to watch *Match of the Day* in embarrassed silence. The second instance was again with Jack, though this time he had a different partner, on a school journey in Surrey. A shed full of straw would make an ideal venue for a spot of how's your father, thought the girls. Thirteen years old they were, like green bananas on the turn. Andy wished for the last three years to rewind so that he could relive them with his newly found knowledge. There was so much he would change, given the chance.

Andy blinked slowly, floated and then something pounded him on the back. Opening his eyes, he stared up at a starry black sky, revolving almost imperceptibly. Resting his head on his chin, he saw that he had pitched over a low wall and landed on somebody's front lawn. The dewy grass was like a moist towel and he rolled over and snuggled into it.

'All right son, on your feet.' There was only one profession in the entire world that instilled in its members such smug self-righteousness. *All* coppers are bastards. 'I said on your feet, son.'

'Fuck orf,' Andy mumbled into his moist towel.

'Don't give me any ag, son, I'm not in the mood. Now shift yerself.' A boot hooked under Andy's ribs and flipped him over. 'Come on,' a fat little face puffed as he was pulled to his feet.

'I told you to fuck orf, didn't I?' Andy pointed his index finger towards where he had imagined the pig's nose would be and somehow managed to miss completely.

The situation was well risky. Any minute now his previous would show up on the computer. Wiggins was gonna love that. And that bastard desk sergeant wasn't helping matters, with his barely concealed hilarity. Still, it was fucking funny.

'You won't be smiling for much longer, mate, I can promise you that.' Police Constable Wiggins waddled over to where Andy sat and leaned into his face. The appalling stench of dried puke wafting off from him almost had Andy throwing up on him again. 'I've already got you for drunk and disorderly, I wonder if there's anything else we could find for you,' he sneered and waddled back to the desk. Apparently the police regulation height had been lowered to include garden gnomes. Dragging the small plastic comb through his lanky hair once more, Wiggins cursed as he hit another snag of tangled knots. Although he'd been in the bog for over ten minutes, he obviously hadn't got rid of it all. A high titter emitted from the sergeant's lips and he glanced anxiously at Wiggins who pretended he hadn't heard. 'All right, son, what were you doing round here? This ain't your manor and you know it.' Wiggins had obviously been boning up on his Sweeney dialogue.

'I was walking. You know, when you put one foot in front of the other. Ring a bell?'

Desperately trying to look hard, Wiggins resembled nothing so much as a spacehopper. 'Don't come it with me, son.'

'I came to see an old girlfriend a' mine,' Andy explained. 'Listen I only knocked your poxy 'at off, didn't even touch ya really.'

'Name?'

'Oh *come* on, wassit matter?'

'Name?' Wiggins spacehopped towards him.

'Shelley Mellors. She lives on Beauf–'

'Oh I know where she lives, all right.' Wiggins rolled back and forth on his heels like a fat skittle. 'The Mellors girl's well known to everyone round here,' he drawled with an apparent air of sarcasm and winked at the sarge, who grinned salaciously. A nail-biting scream sounded from somewhere inside the building. 'Nothing like a night in the cells, is there, lad?' Feeling completely sober, Andy rolled his eyes as another scream erupted. 'You'll have Mad Mary to keep you company.' The blood-curdling shriek couldn't have been bettered in a Hammer film.

But it was the moaning he couldn't stand. Lying there, alone in the dark, Andy was genuinely frightened. Her voice passed through the wall like an aural spectre and hovered over him, stifling him with its awful gloom. And he couldn't help but try and make sense of it.

'Maaahhhh nurrrmmm, maaahhhh eeeeee. Maaa*aahhh* nurrrmmm, maaahhh eeeeee.'

Fourteen

New York reminded Jack of the time the bin men went on strike in London. It was summer and the warm, musky overripe smell was almost edible. Here, it was more of an atmosphere. The buildings and roads seemed to have achieved the perfect state of dilapidation, like a pair of old slippers. The grainy, monochrome feel of late fifties' 'social issue' movies was still here. Union mobster runs down dark alley in the final reel, being chased by his honest cop brother while brash trumpets blare discordantly over a furtive, racing percussion pattern. Otto'd love this place. Everybody on the street looked as though they were in a movie. Now wait a minute, this should've been Third Avenue not Lexington. A man in his late twenties with frizzy hair and tight flared trousers bustled busily towards him.

'Excuse me.'

'Don't hassle me, man.' Putting both hands up to his face, the man seemed to be expecting Jack to produce a camera and take his picture.

'I only wanted to –'

'Yew got prawblems, I got prawblems. We all got prawblems, man, leave me alone.'

'Which way's Third Avenue?' Jack shouted indignantly.

The man stopped in his tracks and whirled around. 'Yew tryin' a' be funny?' He rested his hands on his hips and swaggered provocatively. Maybe he had a gun.

'No – I'm English – can't you tell?' Jack gushed. 'I'm lost. Really.'

'Whaddayew nuts or sump'n? Cary Grant sounds more British

'n yew. Yew wanna hear sump'n? Lissen 'a this.' The man cleared his throat self-consciously and adjusted his crotch. 'Orlright me ol' mucker, ah's yer missus been keepin'? Went dahn the boozer yes'day, got Brahms 'n' Liszt I did, sick as a dog. Yew want British? Dat's British. Don' gimme any "Oi'm English" crap, yew're insultin' my intelligence.' The man bustled away, muttering to himself.

The narrow apartment building smelt of piss, not like the Masons' acrid stench but like the cloying, sweet scent of cheap talcum powder. Lydia's place was on the top floor and by the time he'd reached it, Jack was out of breath. He knocked feebly on the door.

'Who is it? What do you want?'

'My name's Jack Shaw, my father is Ben Shaw, I'm looking for Lydia Ableman.'

A skinny waif with matted brown hair opened the door and ushered him in quickly. She looked like a drowned rat. 'Do I know you?' She glanced up and down the hallway before closing the door.

'No, not really. Your mother is a friend of my father. I'm . . .' Jack watched, fascinated, as the girl grabbed a curved iron pole and jammed one end of it into the lock while the other wedged solidly against the floor a few feet away.

'How did you find me?'

'My father gave me the address. He said you might remember him, though you were only six at the time.'

'Really?' The girl grinned shyly. 'What's your name again?'

'Shaw. Jack Shaw. Son of Ben.'

'Ben Shaw, Ben Shaw, no I can't say – wait a minute – yes, yes of course. Uncle Benjy.'

Benjy? No, that couldn't be right. Ben just wasn't the 'Benjy' type. She must be thinking of someone else.

'And you're his son, wow! You weren't even born when I last saw Uncle Benjy. I remember him saying that he was hoping for a girl.'

'Oh.' Jack had no idea his gender had been a disappointment to anybody.

'So, you've come to the Apple, huh? Where are you staying?'

Surveying the room, Jack could see no connecting doors to other rooms. 'Ahh . . .' He held up a finger and put it to his chin. 'Good point.'

'Sorry about the initial welcome, I'm on edge.' Lydia finished rolling a thin single skinner and lit it. A joint that size wouldn't affect a fly.

'Why?'

She leaned toward him and lowered her voice. 'They're tapping my phone. I'm not sure but I think the apartment may be bugged as well.'

'Why?' Jack was having trouble believing all this, she did seem a trifle neurotic.

After a single toke, Lydia passed the joint. Jack took several deep blasts before passing it back. 'I had a couple a' people here last month. Erm . . . fugitives from justice, you might say.'

'What happened? What did they do?'

'They got out all right. Back in Belfast now.'

'Belfast! You mean –'

Lydia nodded. Without warning Jack's head exploded.

'Look, Jack, I'm pretty busy okay. So I can't show you the sights 'cos I just haven't got the time. All the streets are numbered so it's real easy. If you wanna go uptown, walk toward the Chrysler Building, it's like a silver pagoda. If you wanna go downtown, walk towards the World Trade Center, it's very big and very black. I have a spare mattress or you can sleep with me in my bed, it's up to you. Gotta go now, if the phone rings don't answer it.'

Lydia's one-room apartment was extremely well equipped, with a six-pack of Miller in the fridge, some more of that dynamite weed and a TV. Jack flicked through the TV Guide and found that his favourite sit-com was running five times a day! Who wanted to see the sights?

Something moved in the periphery of his vision and Jack jerked his head around. The greasy, yellowing walls, splattered with random bits of gunge, showed no further signs of movement.

This ganja was really something else, now, back to Felix and Oscar. The overwhelming bias towards advertisements was annoying at first but soon Jack was laughing so hard the commercials came as a welcome chance to get his breath back. And the ads themselves seemed to be getting better, making more sense. What was that? A small dark spot flashed across the corner of his eye. It was obviously a side effect of the smoke, he had to ignore it, get used to it. Kicking off his black suede boots, Jack wiggled his toes inside his fluorescent pink socks.

In between episodes of *The Odd Couple*, he flicked stations and eventually found a programme he liked. At least he thought he did. Four 'celebrities' made up a panel of judges and were stirred on by a deranged MC to insult the acts that appeared. *Opportunity Knocks* with Groucho Marx. One act had a man dressed in a loincloth, lying on a surfboard playing what he assured the panel to be a Peruvian nose flute whilst his wife slapped him on the back and caterwauled her way through 'With a Little Help From My Friends'. At the beginning of the second verse they were gonged off the stage. Towards the end of the show a tiny black boy came on wearing a bowler hat, T-shirt, braces, belt, peg leg turn-ups and spats. Every article of clothing in black or contrasting white. He then proceeded to do a number of freeze-frame poses in time to a funky backtrack. His limbs popped from one position to another with no visible movement in between. He was Joey's age.

Later that afternoon Lydia returned with a man who walked like an upright turtle. His dangling forearms were extraordinarily long and his lower face was fixed in a permanent Goofy 'Gosh' expression.

'Jack, this is my boyfriend, Orson Welles. Orson, this is Jack Shaw, he's a friend of the family.'

'I – I'm sorry, did you say Orson *Welles*?'

'Jeez, where've I heard that before,' said the orang-utan.

'Everybody but everybody gets that wrong the first time. Except me. I didn't, did I Orson?'

'It's Wares, man. You know like "selling my wares". Don't worry, like she said, happens t' everybody.'

135

'Except me, Orson. I got it right the very first time, didn't I?'

Orson flopped into a low armchair and the few remaining springs creaked stiffly. His eyes were set so deep into his head that Jack couldn't tell whether they were looking at him or not. 'So you're in a band, huh?'

'Yeah,' Jack smiled. Being a musician really helped to get over the 'so what do you do?' polite interest because people always seemed genuinely interested.

'I play bass,' Orson drawled.

'Brilliantly,' added Lydia.

With his posture, it should have been obvious.

'Drums.' Jack stuck a thumb into his chest.

'Yeah, I figured. What kinda stuff you like?'

'All kinds of things.'

'Name a few.'

'Reggae, funk, jazz . . .' He winced inwardly at this but it was true, he had sneaked a couple of private listens to Otto's record collection recently.

'Jazz?'

Whoops-a-daisy.

'Like what?'

Too late to back out now. 'Ah . . . Monk, Thelonious Monk. Um . . . oh, whassisname? . . . Mingus, yeah, Charlie Mingus, him.'

'Uh huh.' Orson nodded encouragingly. 'What do you think of Nils Hedding-Pedersen?'

'Ohhhh,' Lydia rolled her eyes to heaven.

That name, it rang a bell. 'Is that the guy with Oscar Peterson, on TV? Stand up?' Jack did a bad mime of someone playing the double bass incredibly fast.

'Yeah, that's right. What a genius. You know what my dream is? To get a bunch a' guys like that and re-record "Pet Sounds" with Spector producing.' Something flickered on the wall. 'Whhhhapp!' In a flash, Orson had scooped Jack's boot off the floor and hurled it. 'Goddamn roaches.'

Retrieving his boot Jack noticed that the greasy spot on the sole more or less matched those on the wall. So that's what it was.

Suddenly he became aware that the floor, the walls, the furniture, the fridge, in fact the whole fucking flat, was crawling.

'See that?' Orson pressed his thumb onto the arm of his chair and then removed it.

Jack stared. 'No.'

'A roach can live off this thumbprint, that you can't even see, for a whole year. If they dropped a nuclear bomb on Manhattan tomorrow, there would be one race guaranteed to survive.'

'The cockroaches,' said Lydia ominously.

Jack was beginning to understand just who this city really belonged to.

'Here, look at this.' Bounding out of his chair Orson pulled out what looked like a doll's house from underneath the sink. Printed in large letters on the side were the words 'Roach Motel'. 'Take a look.'

Through a rectangular hole in the roof Jack saw a sea of shiny, undulating cockroaches.

'There's some yellow stuff on the floor that smells good and when they go in they get stuck to it.'

The 'footwear as guided missile' method seemed a lot more humane. 'I'd like to hear you play. What's the name of your group?'

'Haven't thought of one yet. We're rehearsing over on Fourteenth Street in an hour. Come along, the guys won't mind.'

Lydia wasn't invited.

Jack got the feeling that the guys did mind. One of them anyway. Doug Luck was the singer, song-writer, saxophonist and supposed sex symbol of the group. No vague pretence of democracy here, it was strictly his show. The music was odd to say the least. Orson and Dan, the drummer, laid down a tricky, twitching funk groove while Luck screeched over the top either vocally or instrumentally, it didn't seem to make much difference, like a strangled chicken. Amongst all this, Steph and Nina played slide guitar and organ respectively as though they were in a completely different band playing a completely different song. But at the end of each number they all finished simultaneously so they obviously knew what they were doing. The rehearsal came to an abrupt end when Luck flounced out of the room and did not return.

'That was great,' Jack enthused as the group began to pack away.

'Hey thanks,' said Steph, or was it Nina. 'Something was bothering Doug, though. He wasn't on very good form today.'

'How could you tell?' asked Jack, dropping the brick before he could stop himself.

Rain splashed the sidewalk and steam rose from the mysterious manhole covers in the middle of the road. Perhaps there were dragons in the sewer.

A strangely spherical cat scurried along the gutter and Orson jumped back from the kerb. 'Fuck! Did you see the size of that fucking thing?'

'What was it?' asked Jack timidly, sensing something unpleasant.

'It was a goddamn water rat, biggest fucking thing I've ever seen.'

A rat? No way. It was five times bigger than a rat. Jack imagined a comparable cockroach and shuddered at the thought.

The shiny, black road surface was like a dirty mirror, hazily reflecting the neon signs and street lamps. Somehow, the artificial light was much more real than the natural daylight. The vapid, pale yellow cabs became a deep and vibrant orange and the myriad shadows gave even the most nondescript fire hydrant an atmospheric aura.

'Wanna shoot some pool?'

Mario's was heaven on earth. The entire first floor of a gigantic warehouse had been converted to accommodate some twenty-five to thirty pool tables. And these were no ordinary tables. Full size, seven and a half feet long, with immaculately maintained sky-blue baize. For five dollars they were going to have two hours of uninterrupted bliss. No drunks, no amateurs, no women, just pool, glorious pool. If only he'd had the foresight to bring his coveted cue, what a great place this would be to christen it.

At first, Jack's ignorance of American rules put him a few frames behind, which was perfect as it became clear that he was the slightly better player.

'What's happening with you and Lydia?' asked Jack, missing an easy double into the middle pocket.

'Unlucky.' Orson crouched down and closed one eye, trying to judge the angle of his next shot. 'She comes around, sometimes I wanna see her, sometimes I don't.' The shot missed by a mile and the wandering cue ball nudged a difficult stripe away from the side cushion leaving Jack with a clear field.

'I only asked because . . .' He rammed the first ball home.

'Take my advice, man, check to see if she's clean first. I had to go the whole of last summer without a drink, trying a' shake that pox.' Orson tutted as the second ball slammed against the back of the corner pocket and jumped out again. 'Take it easy, Jack. There is such a thing as hitting the ball too hard.'

The stores, like the TV, were doing business twenty-four hours a day and the dealer lived in the apartment below so, armed with a six-pack and a spliff, Jack got to grips with America. The days blurred together in a slow dissolve. One afternoon, Lydia showed up.

'Hi, where have you been?' With some effort, Jack raised himself and turned off the TV.

'Euggghh!' Lydia's jaw dropped. Jack had become an effective marksman and the greasy spots on the wall had increased rather noticeably. 'This is disgusting, how can you live like this?'

It was true, the whole flat had degererated somewhat. Crumpled beer cans lay next to half-smoked joints and the olive on that slice of pizza was definitely moving.

'Let's get outta here, huh? I'll show you New York.'

The weather was cold, not surprisingly for the time of year.

'The boat leaves from West Forty-Second. I've never been on it myself. It's a good time to go, there won't be too many tourists. Do you mind walking? It's a long way but I love to walk.'

'Me too.' It would give him a chance to warm up. Suddenly, a thought struck him. 'What's the date?'

'It's New Year's Eve.' They'd been mentioning it every five minutes on TV but he hadn't made the connection until now.

'December thirty-first. I'm going home tomorrow.'

The boat sailed all the way around Manhattan Island. Thirteen miles long and so skinny you could look down a street and see clear to the other side. It was like having the best part of London cut out and dumped in the sea. As usual on these things, you had to be a politician or a businessman to get a mention in the tour guide's rambling monologue about who lived where and built what.

'And as we move into the hundreds we come to the district known as Harlem. The Harlem River becomes very narrow at this point and, as you can see, Manhattan almost touches with the Bronx. Obviously there is a strong connection between these two areas but the public image of Harlem can be very misleading. The portrayal of Harlem we see on television and in the movies is often a biased and inaccurate one. The Museum of the City of New York and the Cathedral of St John the Divine are just two of the historic landmarks situated in this area. For many years Harlem has been the breeding ground for innovative artists such as Duke –'

From out of nowhere, a bottle flew through the air and smashed across the back of the tour guide's head, knocking him down. On the footbridge above them, a young black kid jumped up and down, whooping and hollering.

'And this,' Lydia raised her arms proudly, 'is the best restaurant in the world.'

The Second Avenue Deli didn't sound like much, but she turned out to be correct nevertheless. A chicken salad sandwich seemed to consist of an entire chicken, half a pound of every vegetable known to man smothered in mayonnaise, and two halves of a family-sized loaf. Having already helped himself to one of the free mega-gherkins swimming in brine, Jack couldn't finish it. One sandwich.

'Have you been seeing Orson at all?'

'Who's been talking?' asked Lydia, accidentally spraying chopped liver onto Jack's plate. 'Sorry,' she swallowed.

'It's okay, I've finished.'

'Yeah? Would you mind?'

'Go ahead.' Jack watched as she shovelled the remains of his meal onto her own mountainous pile of food.

'We have an agreement. He can stay with me or I can stay with him but we're keeping both apartments. We have to have that freedom. Do you have a girl?'

'I came three thousand miles to see one and she said it wasn't the right time, could I come back later?' He let out a hollow laugh.

'I wouldn't do that for anyone. Not unless I really loved them.'

A tall, thin, spindly old lady doddered over to their table. She wore a pristine pink uniform and a little white bonnet. 'Excuse my natural curiosity, I couldn't help but overhear. Am I in the presence of an Englishman?'

'Yes, I'm from London, actually,' said Jack, wanting to avoid the conversational pitfall he had encountered with Señor Loco.

'Oh that's really quite amazing. A coincidence, even, I should say. My sister, when she was nineteen, emigrated. Over forty years ago already.' The waitress paused for a moment.

'To London?'

'Yes, uh huh. On Upper Street she has a house and two cats. The neighbours, she says, are nice, clean people. Mrs Rosen. Number fourteen. You've met perhaps?'

'No, I'm afraid not. You see . . .' It was no good. The waitress was visibly heartbroken.

'Could we get a couple of doggies?' asked Lydia and the waitress limped off.

'Doggies?'

'Yeah, doggy bags, you know, for the food you can't finish. You're supposed to take it home for your dog so they're called doggy bags.'

What a great idea. Mrs Rosen's sister came back holding two paper containers with cardboard handles.

'Enjoy. Come again.'

'I'll pick up the tab on this one,' Lydia announced.

'Why can't we go Dutch?' asked Jack, not really wanting to.

'Because right now, I have more money than you do. Next time I see you, things might be different.'

Fifteen

'Nah,' Andy lied in answer to Grace's question asking whether he had his own phone. 'Anyway, what's 'app'nin' today? Where we gonna go?'

'Aah, a problem. You see my sister's come up for a couple of days.'

There was a long silence. Was she lying to him? Andy wished he was talking to her face to face.

'Hold on,' said Grace and there was a clunk as she put the receiver down. After a minute or so the pips went and Andy fumbled in his back pocket for another ten pence. 'Okay,' she said, picking up again, 'this is the plan. I'm taking Angie to lunch at Harrods and then she's going to toddle off to the museums. Honestly, my family, the culture vultures.' The laughter in the background sounded distinctly unfeminine. Could've been Otto but why would *he* be laughing? 'I'll come over to your place at about two thirty, okay?'

'Er . . . no. Let's meet in the . . .' where? . . . 'the Golden Lion, Fulham Broadway, it's more sort of on your way.' It wasn't at all. 'Two firty, you said. Can't wait to see the motor.'

She looked a right state. A ragged woollen skirt and knee-length nylon socks covered most of her bandy legs, but not quite. The two podgy pillars were absolutely rampant with fuzzy growth. Her left tit hung over the body of the bass guitar like a balloon full of water, undulating unpleasantly as she waggled her leg in time to the beat. '*I'm fat, a snail without a shell, living hell. I'm fat –'* No argument there, love, but why bother setting it to music?

Grace bounded out of the ladies. 'Je suis prête.' The singer scowled at them as they walked in front of the small, slightly raised stage and out into the lemon yellow sunlight. 'Isn't it gorgeous?'

'Fuckin' ace.' Like a pair of jet black shades, the car was cool.

'You can see out but no one can see in, it's amazing isn't it?' Grace enthused gleefully.

'Fuckin' ace,' Andy repeated, unable to top the superlative.

'Get in,' she said and unlocked the near-side door before walking around and letting herself in. 'You'll find a knob under the seat.'

'Do what?' Andy said astonishedly, remembering the contents of Grace's dressing table drawer.

'A knob, you just push it up and slide back as far as you want.'

'Ay?'

'If you need more room. For your legs.'

Feeling underneath his seat, Andy found the button and the seat shot backwards. He stretched out his long legs and sank back into the leather upholstery. Or was it plastic? Whatever.

The Mini sped towards Hampstead Road and the Heath. It wasn't exactly beside the sea but there you go. The Capital Radio building flashed by on the left.

'What does Jack get up to during the day?'

'Not much, this and that. I don't know, why?'

'I just wondered if 'e 'ad much spare time.'

'Bags, I should think. He and Otto seem to spend most of the day sitting around getting smashed. To be fair though, they have been pretty busy recently, what with the auditions.' Andy's heart skipped a beat. 'They're looking for a new singer, I thought of putting my name forward but apparently they're only interested in men. I'm too bloody good for them anyway.'

'Yeah,' Andy agreed absent-mindedly.

'It's a shame I haven't got a voice like Angie's, they'd probably hire me on the spot. She's got the lowest range of any woman I've ever heard and it just seems to get deeper all the time. You must meet her before she goes back, I'm sorry you can't stay with me tonight but, you know, older sisters. Andy?'

'Huh?'

'Hmmh,' Grace purred, 'honestly, that stunt you pulled on the train . . . We would have had to pay your fare, you know. It wasn't as though you could get off at Golders Green or something, the train didn't stop until Huntingdon, miles away. *Hon*estly.'

The Music Machine loomed in the distance. How long before he stood on that venue's stage with the roar of the crowd ringing in his ears? Of course, they'd have to change the name. And the clothes. And the music.

'I came here last autumn to pick mushrooms,' said Grace as they walked, hand in hand, across the vast green expanse.

'I've never been keen, meself.'

'Really? I love them. They're not at all like acid, they're much more natural and pure. You get a wonderful feeling of, I don't know, it's like everything is just . . . wonderful.'

'What are you on about?' Andy asked, baffled.

'Magic mushrooms.'

'*Magic* mushrooms. What do they do, card tricks? Magic mushrooms,' he repeated mockingly.

They walked silently, their feet squelching into the moist grass. Several dogs barked, both near and far away, in expressive morse code. They had no idea that the year was coming to a close and that they should be making resolutions about how to be better dogs. Like vowing to stop shitting on the pavement when they knew damn well it was against the law. 'What day is it?' he asked.

'New Year's Eve.'

'No I mean what *day* is it?'

'Umm . . . Sunday I th– no, Saturday. Why?'

'I just wondered.' They squelched on.

'– and that's why I said it, do you see? I didn't want to give you the wrong impression because after all when two people –' And on and on she went.

From what Andy could decipher from the past fifteen minutes of gobbledy-gook, Grace loved him but she didn't. Simple as that. The word sex had cropped up many, many times, reflecting their main activity together, and she was trying to differentiate between it and love. It seemed clear enough to Andy. Love was something you felt for your family, your wife, your dog, your cat, your job, roast beef and Yorkshire pudding or Peter Osgood's hat tricks. Sex was when you had a bang and shot yer load.

'– so it isn't that I don't love you, because I do. Do you see?'

'Sure.'

'Do you really?'

'Absolutely.'

'Do you love me?'

'I love 'avin' sex wiv ya,' he laughed. They both did. 'So I s'pose that means I love you. Except for that scab on yer bum.'

'What scab?' Grace cried and jerked around, clutching at her behind. 'Oh ha ha, very funny.'

'I thought so.' Her bum, like the rest of her skin, was flawless. She'd really worked up a sweat in the car and Andy had thought the suspension was gonna go any minute. If it weren't for the fact that the grass was wet, they'd probably be doing it here as well. Andy tried to imagine the most unlikely place they could do it and came to an obvious conclusion. His own bed.

Grace was shocked.

'It's absolutely outrageous, you can't just throw someone in jail for no reason. You should sue them.'

'Well, I did throw up on 'im.'

'Only because he punched you in the stomach, *God* it makes me so angry.'

'Well, I did knock 'is 'elmet off first.'

Grace guffawed helplessly. 'I suppose you did do that. Still it serves him right. Was he really that short?'

'On my life,' Andy placed his hand on his heart, ''e looked as though someone'd dropped an anvil on 'is 'ead, like in one a' them Tom and Jerry cartoons.'

'Hah,' Grace exploded and the Mini swerved to the left, narrowly missing a parked car.

'Anyway, it turned out all right. I reckon the sarge must've talked 'im out of it. They could've 'ad me for D and D, no danger. I dunno about assault but wiv my previous . . .' He shuddered to think. Prison, definitely, more than ninety days an' all. Yep, he'd been lucky all right.

Walking into the upstairs bar in the Roebuck, Andy wished they'd stayed downstairs. The punks, ponces and poofs up here made him nervous. The sight of Otto, sitting at the far end in one of the chairs surrounding the pool tables, was one for sore eyes. Andy ordered the drinks and Grace paid for them. 'I can't stay long,' she said as they made their way over to Otto, 'I'm meeting Angie back at the flat –'

'At seven, I know.' That suited Andy just fine because he had a few things he wanted to ask Otto, in private.

'I thought you were going to a party tonight,' said Grace.

'That's right,' Otto replied.

'I'm surprised Adam didn't invite me. I expect he thought I'd still be away.'

'Hmm. I'm sure he wouldn't mind if you came along.'

'Oh no, not without being invited.'

Andy tried to recall how many parties he had crashed and decided, whatever the amount, it was certainly a fuck of a lot more than he'd been invited to.

'Suit yourself.'

'I will.'

'Did you have a good Christmas?' Otto asked Andy.

'Mustn't grumble. You?'

'Pretty quiet, I guess. It's the first one I've had without my parents and . . . I don't know . . . it was weird, you know?'

'I can't imagine Christmas without my family,' said Grace.

'Yeah well, there's bound to come a day when . . .'

'I don't see why.'

'Well say you're abroad or they're abroad then –'

'Then we'd all have to make an extra effort, I wouldn't let that stop me.'

At eight fifteen, Otto rose from his chair.

"Old up,' Andy insisted, 'it's my round.' It was time to start pumping him about the band. Had they found a singer yet? Did they have a certain sort of person in mind? And, after he'd ordered a couple of bottles of Brew instead of the piss Otto was drinking, did Andy, by any chance, fit the bill?

'No thanks, I'd better get going.'

'A quick 'alf, go on,' Andy implored.

'No really, I must be off, I'm meeting someone at eight thirty.'

'Christine McArfur,' Andy stated confidently.

'Yeah.' Otto blinked rapidly. 'How did you know?'

'Just guessed.' Perhaps he'd been wrong about her sexual preference, either that or Otto didn't know about it yet. 'That's a bit of all right, innit? I should fink your next single can't fail, what wiv you *and* Jack bein' in the band.' Otto grimaced. 'I wonder what Jack'll say when 'e gets back?'

'I think I will have that drink.'

'So,' Andy continued as they walked over to the bar, 'Grace tells me you're lookin' for a singer.'

'Yeah, do you know anybody? I mean anybody good? I've had it up to here with time-wasters. You should see some of the dickheads we've had to put up with. Of course, you can't throw them out of the audition after one song, oh no, you have to give them a chance.' His eyes widened and his cheeks inflated as he let out an exhausted sigh. 'There was one girl – cheers,' he sipped his beer, 'she was absolutely stunning. Our tongues were on the floor, even Alex, that's our bass player. Jack,' he laughed, 'Jack went through two pairs of drumsticks while she auditioned, I've never seen him hit those drums so hard. It was so tempting, you know, to ask her to join. We could've had every newspaper in the country running after us with a face like that up front but,' he snorted and smiled ruefully, 'the voice, Jesus Christ, it was like listening to someone being circumcised without an anaesthetic.'

Having no idea that Otto could be so cruelly animated, Andy began to drop his bottle. 'I fought you was looking for blokes.'

Otto let his chin sag to his chest in a sign of total defeat. 'I tell you man, it's unbelievable, we've auditioned – what? – thirty maybe, and out of all those guys not one of them was any use. There's two types, see, the heavy metal screamers who still expect the drummer to do a fifteen minute solo in the middle of the set, while they do a costume change, and the J.R. clones. I don't want the group to end up sounding exactly like the Pistols – I mean what's the point in that? Anyway, I'm thinking of changing the ad to something more 'pacific like er . . . "Young band with recording contract requires" . . . er . . . I don't know, something that'll put off all the wankers. I tell you, if we don't pull our finger out, there won't *be* a bloody recording contract.'

Since Otto was heading for Parson's Green, Andy cadged a lift to the bottom of the King's Road.

"Ow come you and Grace split up?' Grace's drug excuse didn't hold much water. It was an odd question to be asking, given that they still shared the same flat. 'You still seem to get on all right. I couldn't imagine livin' wiv a bird 'oo I'd been out wiv before. But you two seem to get on all right.'

Otto did not reply.

The black labrador sniffed at Andy's feet and raised its leg in preparation to pee. The dog howled as Andy jerked the toe of his DM up into its balls.

"Ere don't do that,' Brenda protested, 'what's 'e ever done to you? You big bully.'

They sat side by side on Andy's park bench. He wished she'd go away and leave him to think in peace. An empty fag packet skittered past in the wind and the dog bolted after it.

'So what you been up to?' she asked.

'Wassit to you?'

'Oh charmin', I'm sure. What's the matter wiv you then? Someone take away your teddy bear, did they?'

'Leave it out, Brenda. Go an' pick on someone your own size, will ya?'

'No, why should I? It's a free country. I've got just as much right to sit 'ere as what you 'ave.'

He couldn't argue with that. He tried to think of something to say that would make her go away.

''Ere Andy?'

'What?' he responded exasperatedly.

'I can fart wiv' me cunt, wanna 'ear it?'

'Gordon Bennett, Bren, give it a rest. I wanna be by myself, all right?'

'Why?'

'Wassit matter why? Why would I want to 'ear Brenda Royce and 'er amazing farting fanny?' A slimy, bubbling raspberry emitted from Brenda's lower regions. Andy absolutely refused to be amused by this childish display. Another pocket of air oozed audibly out of her vaginal orifice. 'I'm warnin' you, Bren, j–'

''S great innit?'

'Oh yeah, triffic. Wiv a bit of practice I 'spect you'll be able to play the National Anthem.'

'Ooh, I dunno about that. Do you fink so? I can do it in time to a beat, listen.'

'*No*,' Andy threw up his hands in alarm, 'I believe ya, all right? Fuck me,' he breathed heavily.

The labrador trotted back towards them and sat patiently at Brenda's side. A flock of seagulls shrieked and cawed overhead and the labrador studied them with great interest, unable to fathom just exactly why he was down here while they were up there.

'Wanna feel me tits?' she offered casually.

Andy rolled his eyes. 'What is the matter with you?'

'Me? It's you 'oo's got the 'ump.'

'Why? Just 'cos I don't wanna squeeze your ruddy tits? Strewf, Bren, you must 'ave somethin' better to do than goin' round askin' geezers to feel you up.'

'I didn't say feel me up I just s–'

'I know, I know but look, there are other fings in life besides all that.'

'Like what?'

'Whaddya mean like what? Like everyfing.'

'Like what?'

Examining the telephone apparatus carefully, Andy decided that he was very, very drunk. Paralytic. There were three 10p slots instead of the usual one so he closed his right eye and the slot on the left disappeared. Then he closed his left eye and they all disappeared, as did everything else, and he lost his balance, banged his forehead and collapsed into a heap in the corner.

'Arright mon, right ya self.' Andy grabbed the black man's hand and was lifted to his feet. 'Trine a' call a bredren, ee? Seh wh' 'appen fe me. Ites.' The man disappeared.

The whole phone booth did a twisting somersault. Or was it the world outside? Trafalgar Square on New Year's Eve was a sight to behold, except that right now, he was having great difficulty beholding anything at all. Hordes of people scurried and flopped like otters, some darting between moving vehicles in the middle of the road, others splashing up and down in the fountain on the square. Grace. Yes. Must phone Grace, say Happy New Year. Andy tried to ram the coin into the slot but it wouldn't go. Confusion. Wassapp'nin'? The number, oh yeah, dial the number. Andy dialled the number.

'Seven oh five one, who's calling please?'

'Oohsis?' Andy demanded.

'Seven oh five one, can I help you?'

'Otto? You're not 'im, are ya? Oohsis?'

'I'm afraid he's out at the moment, can I take a mess–? Hold on a second.'

'Ay? 'Oo *is* sis?'

'Hello? Otto's not here at the moment. I can give you the number of where he is if you–' said Grace.

'*Oyyyy!*' Andy bellowed, ''s me, innit? Andy.'

'Andy you sound completely paralytic.'

'Ha haaa, ha haa ha.'

'What's going on? Where are you?'

'No, no, I'm 'avin' a wonderful time, in fact, I've been told to say 'ello to you by a very nice man 'oo 'elped me up.'

'Helped you up? What man? Andy, where are you?'

151

'Actually, 'e was one of your lot.'

'My lot?'

'Yeah, you know, a coloured geezer.'

'And –'

'I've got nuffin' against 'em, you know – well you *know* that, don't ya?'

'Andy, for God's sake,' she snapped, 'where are you? What's going on?'

"Ere,' said Andy and opened the door, 'cop a load a' this.' Holding the receiver out into the cold night air, he hoped that the horns, whistles, bells, screams and shouts would be audible on the other end of the line. 'Switch yer telly on and in . . .' He looked at his watch. It was five hundred and fifty-two minutes past a hundred and eleven. '. . . any moment now, you'll see me. I'll be in the fountain.'

'Trafalgar Square?'

'Ayyy.' Bursting into spontaneous applause, Andy dropped the phone. Bending down to retrieve it, he careered head first into the door and landed back down on his arse. The dangling receiver swung towards him and he caught it.

'Hello, Andy?'

'Yeah, I'm still h–'

'Beep beep beep beep –' Sod it. '– beep beep beep beep –' Okay okay, keep yer 'air on. '– beep beep beep beeeeeee –'

Sixteen

What in God's name had happened to him? Chrissy went to the window once more and peered up and down the street. She'd spent an entire hour putting her brand new, grey trilby on, and taking it off again, every time a light blue car went by and turned out not to contain Otto. It was bad luck to wear a hat indoors.

A sky blue Citroën nosed past the window. At last. The car cruised slowly down the street in search of a parking space.

Staring critically at herself in a full-length mirror, Chrissy still couldn't decide whether to tilt the trilby forwards or backwards. With the brim down over one eye, she looked a little sluttish. But with the hat sitting back on her head, she looked like Chico Marx. Or perhaps it was the raincoat.

Hurriedly, she unbuttoned the raincoat and grabbed a three-quarter length leather coat from the hatstand. The more pedantic carnivores, feeling guilty about their own contribution to the destruction of animal life, would feel it their duty to point out that slaughtering cows in order to obtain leather was no less unnecessary than turning them into hamburgers. It was a theory that Chrissy couldn't argue with, but right now as she gave her appearance the final once over, she couldn't give a – oh no, teeth, she'd forgotten to brush her blessed teeth. Thrashing the brush around her mouth, Chrissy poked out her tongue and scraped away the whatever-it-was that always seemed to collect there. The doorbell chimed. Rushing towards the door, she stopped for one last look in the mirror. The trilby was definitely a mistake and she took it off before opening the door.

Tucked just behind Harrods, the old Edwardian square looked as though it had leapt through a time warp into the present day. They circled the gardens in the centre of the square several times. Parson's Green was only up and coming compared to this. Half the houses in the square were foreign embassies and the rest undoubtedly had their basements designated as servants' quarters. There's always somebody better off than you are. As they purred around the gardens again, Chrissy wished they could stay like this forever. Going round and round and never having to stop or get out.

'What the fuck?' The car screamed to the left as Otto span the steering wheel one hundred and eighty degrees.

Something sailed in front of them, the physical appearance of which Chrissy could not quite believe. She blinked hard.

'Where's your helmet, you crazy son of a bitch?' Otto yelled at the top of his voice. 'Look at him, the stupid fucker. The man's a complete maniac. Adam,' he shrieked, 'for Chrissakes, man, get down from there. You'll do yourself an injury.'

Standing on the seat of his motorbike on one leg, with the other stretched out at a right angle behind him, Adam continued his ballet on wheels and revved up to sixty.

'Is that –' In front of them, the bike began zig-zagging from one side of the road to the other. 'Is that for our benefit?' Chrissy asked in amazement.

'Shouldn't think so,' Otto laughed and stamped on the foot brake. 'Fuck it, I've had enough of this. I'll leave the address on the windscreen. If this guy wants to get out he can come and get me.'

The car hissed and sank a few inches as the suspension relaxed. Stepping out, Chrissy held her door open as Otto wiggled across the seats, his own door being obstructed by a Bentley. Speedway's answer to Nureyev glided gracefully past them and disappeared out of the square.

'Is he coming to the party?' Was it likely that a man would drive around a square in Knightsbridge for no reason at all? And in such a peculiar fashion.

'I hope so,' Otto chuckled. 'It's his party.'

So this was what she'd been missing all those years. It was like a real life recreation of one of those party sequences in a sixties' movie. The kind that nobody believed really happened. Her attention was caught immediately by the large cups filled with ready rolled joints that were dotted around the room. Everybody seemed to be helping themselves, so Chrissy did the same. She turned to Otto who held out a lighted match and smiled.

'Nice touch,' she said, having to raise her voice only slightly above the smooth instrumental jazz-funk.

The floor was littered with people, many of whom were lying down, too zonked to do anything else. The atmosphere was completely relaxed and, though she recognised one or two faces from the Roebuck, there was none of that venue's underlying aggression evident here. Cross-legged in the middle of the surrounding chaos, a young boy sat looking blankly innocent. He was far too young to be witnessing all this. Chrissy tugged at Otto's elbow. 'Who's that wee boy? He looks lost.'

Otto followed her gaze. 'Oh don't worry about Dom. He knows how to look after himself.'

As if on cue, the boy produced a large lump of hashish and began picking off flakes and scattering them into a pile of tobacco in front of him.

'Good Lord. How old is he? He can't be more than –'

'Thirteen,' Otto agreed.

It was incredible. 'Do his parents know he's here?'

Mumbling greetings to a small hairy person of indeterminate sex, Otto turned his head. 'What?'

'I said do his parents know he's –'

'Who, Dom? Yeah sure, they're right over there.' He pointed to a group of horizontal zombies. 'They wouldn't let anything happen to him. He's the only one in the family who earns any money.'

'You're kidding?'

'No I'm not. He's a dealer. Oh yeah, that reminds me. I want to pay you back for the other night. You said you fancied some smoke.'

Leading a dumbfounded Chrissy by the hand, Otto negotiated them both through the human debris and they knelt down next to the boy. His pure, clear, dewy-eyed expression remainded her of a choirboy.

'How's it going, Dom?'

'Business is booming, dear boy. Might I interest you and your ladyfriend in some of these?' From his shirt pocket the boy produced a thin strip of paper decorated with pictures of Donald Duck. 'The finest lysergic acid blotters money can buy. One of these can last for up to eight hours. Take two and you can have that weekend trip right there in your very own home. I took three about a week ago and man, I tell you. I still haven't come back. Wanna know what colour you are right now? Tartan. I swear to God, if you could see what I'm seeing, you'd wig out.' All at once the boy's pupils dilated so much they almost filled his entire iris. 'I kid you not, man, I kid you not,' he chanted in an eerie monotone to no one in particular and stared off into space.

'Er, yeah. Listen, Dom, we'd like to buy some smoke. Any chance?'

'This year I was smart.' The boy's tone became normal again but he continued to stare straight ahead. 'I've been stockpiling my best gear since September. You remember the trouble I had getting anything this time last year?'

Last year! The boy's voice hadn't even broken.

He came out of his trance and turned to face them. 'What's the difference,' he said and snickered impishly. 'What's the difference between Sherlock Holmes and Walt Disney?' Turning away again, the boy rubbed his chin thoughtfully as though it was he who had been asked the question.

'I don't know, Dom, what is the difference between Sherlock Holmes and Walt Disney?' Otto asked impatiently.

'Well, Sherlock Holmes smokes a pipe but Walt,' he paused and snickered again, 'Disney.'

Chrissy gurgled with glee and choked on the smoke from the joint. Meanwhile Otto sat silently mouthing the words 'Walt Disney' and frowning. The fact that he didn't get it made the joke even funnier and her chest heaved and wheezed as she gasped for air. Otto glanced at Chrissy, twirled his finger around his temple and pointed the finger at an oblivious Dom. She collasped into giggles and the more she tried to regain control of herself, the less easy it became.

Calmly, Dom began to reel off his list of wares. 'I got gold Leb, double zero Moroccan, Afghani black, Paki black and a few of those Nepalese temple balls, specially impregnated with opium. You know, those little white flecks you get on the inside?'

'That's opium?'

'Yeah, you bet. As far as weed goes, I've got Jamaican sensi, just off the boat, plus a few Thai sticks. The Durban poison's run out, man. Sorry about that.'

'I can't talk to you now, man, I'm busy. What was it you wanted to talk about?' Adam's chin was shaped like a ski jump. There was an electric buzz about him. Even when he remained stationary, which wasn't often or for long, his molecules bubbled like the balls in a bingo game. He was a sculpture student at the Royal College of Art but had been suspended for punching one of the caretakers. Apparently they took exception to him destroying his own work. In a grubby 1940s' zoot suit with box shoulders and massive lapels, his stringy, angular body gave him a bionic-Byronic appearance. Time was evidently running much too slowly for him and he delivered his words at the speed of light. The Adam Chrissy was seeing was probably a delayed image and, in fact, the real Adam had already beamed forward to next Tuesday. 'It's not that I don't want to talk to you. It's just that I can only talk about certain things at the moment. Things that are important to me. Important things.' His face pleaded to be understood. 'Otherwise I'll have to go and talk to somebody else. You have to be in the same dimension to–to–to–'

'Communicate?' offered Chrissy.

Adam's eyes lit up. 'Okay, yeah – yeah – we're rolling. Communication. Yeah – yeah – that's it exactly. I'm Adam and you're. . . ?'

Chrissy resisted the temptation to say Eve. 'Christine.'

'No. No you're not,' Adam snapped. 'I know who you are. Miss Communication. Mass Communication.'

Though his conversational tangents were not immediately graspable, there was pure logic in there somewhere.

'Tell me something,' he begged her, 'Tell me something I don't know.'

Chrissy thought for a moment. 'My age?'

'Yes – yes – that's it, good. Tell me your age.'

'Thirty-seven,' she lied, inexplicably.

'Thirty-seven. Three and seven equals ten. One and nought equals one. Therefore you are one,' he stated industriously. 'You're the same age as me, I'm nineteen. Nine and one, ten. One and nought . . . we share the same predicament. Now Otto here, he's twenty. Can't you tell? Can't you just see it? He's a two. Isn't it obvious?'

Yes it was.

The stereo hummed faintly and somebody cleared their throat. Apart from that, the room was silent. Monstrous shadows flickered on the walls like evil spirits. Chrissy sat on a chair in the middle of the room surrounded by curious, half-lit faces. How had she let herself get into this? Adam was a silver-tongued serpent. Wetting his thumb and forefinger, Otto extinguished another candle.

'Okay, perfect,' said Adam, satisfied with the new lighting arrangement. 'Now, we need two volunteers. Women, I think, just to make it more interesting.'

Women. Oh Lord, she'd naturally assumed that the feat would have to be performed by men. Suddenly she felt pinned and tied to the chair by the assembled party goers' collective stare. If she tried to get up, her legs would simply collapse beneath her. Cold sweat trickled down both sides of her torso.

'Come on, we haven't got all night,' Adam coaxed.

No one showed any sign of wanting actively to participate.

'There's nothing to worry about, it's completely safe. Dominic. How about you?' Adam asked, evidently reasoning that the boy would make a passable surrogate female.

158

'I can't go through with this,' Chrissy blurted and her knees began to tremble violently.

'Nonsense,' Adam declared. 'Dom, come and give us a hand.'

Chrissy closed her eyes and tried to wake up from the dream she knew she wasn't having.

'All right then, let's get on with it,' announced a bold female voice.

Even in that light, the girl's flaming red hair made her look as though she'd been plugged in. Facially she bore a great resemblance to Adam but where his eyes had a definite streak of insanity, hers glowed with pure intelligence. She was dressed as if she might have brought Tarzan along. With an outfit like that, Chrissy couldn't imagine how she hadn't noticed the girl before.

'Hi, I'm Erica. I don't think we've met.' The girl shook Chrissy's limp, sweaty hand firmly. 'You look scared. Don't be. I've seen Adam do this a million times. Mind you, there was that one time when Jack bashed his head on the ceiling.'

A wave of nostalgic laughter rippled around the room.

The trick worked and, though it wasn't magic, Chrissy still couldn't figure out how they'd done it.

First, Adam faffed around with a lot of hype and hocus-pocus. Holding his hand just above her head, he asked the other three to stack their hands, one by one, on top of his but without touching each other. Then he asked them to concentrate. On what? A strange feeling of giddiness had come over Chrissy at that point but, since everyone in the room was holding their breath in anticipation, it was hardly surprising. Adam slipped a forefinger under the back of her right knee while Otto took the left. Dom and Erica had the rather more unpleasant task of inserting their digits underneath her streaming armpits. With these four single fingers they proposed to lift nine stone of Yorkshire pudding. Psychologically, things were in their favour as they were under the impression that she only weighed eight and a half.

Adam announced that he would count to five and immediately began doing so. On 'three', Chrissy uttered the nearest thing she ever would to a primal scream. In order to do the trick, it was vital that each henchman knew in advance that they were to lift on 'three'. And the victim couldn't be anybody who'd seen the trick before. Very neat. But it still didn't explain how she had suddenly found herself suspended six feet above the ground, howling like a maniac, with four Peter Pointers as her only visible means of support.

The journey back down to Earth wasn't quite so smooth. Apparently once the victim was aware that the impossible is happening, it tended to stop happening.

Erica, it transpired, was Adam's twin sister and the way Otto's eyes burned into her from time to time indicated a certain history between them. They'd make an ideal couple. The four of them sat around the kitchen table together with Dom.

'Ahhhhh. '78, here we come. Thanks a lot, Adam.' Otto slid the mirror along to Chrissy.

Long lines of white powder ran parallel with each other. She had actually tried coke once before, at Julia's behest, so it didn't come as too much of a shock when the front half of her face went completely numb.

'I feel as though someone's just dropped an iron helmet over my head.' Although the statement was absolutely accurate, she had meant it to remain a silent thought. The others laughed. 'You know, I've just had a great idea. Why don't we all drive off somewhere?'

'Anywhere in particular?' asked Adam.

Great. If he was enthusiastic, then Otto was sure to come. But that was a good question. Where? They could drive down to the south coast and – no. Some people had to work tomorrow and she happened to be one of them. The countryside, yes. They could find an old inn off the beaten track and – no. Too quiet. It had to be somewhere exciting. Somewhere with lots of energy and – and – movement. Like a journey – a continuous, high speed –

'We could go to Heathrow,' said Adam. 'I'll take you on the back of my bike.'

That was it – that was it exactly. Thrashing along the motorway at a hundred miles an hour with the wind roaring in your ears and only the ability to hold on tight standing between you and – no.

Riding with Adam was like asking Charles Manson to supper.

'Does anyone have a cigarette?' The Marlboro went down like a menthol. She wanted another.

'Sure.' Otto tapped out another from the soft pack.

'Should auld acquaintance be forgot and hum de-dum dum dum.' Chrissy had never learnt the words.

'Da dee de-dum, da dee de-dum, for the sake of auld lang syne.' Otto obviously didn't know the words either but, like her, he was still quite willing to perform his dummy lyrics with gusto.

Adam's friends were a weird bunch. Many of them had gone to the same public school which was, in Adam's own words, for Eton rejects whose families had a lot of money. They were well spoken, had parents who lived in the countryside and girlfriends called Amanda and Rebecca. There was something unreal about them.

'Champagne,' Adam barked and clapped his hands twice.

Still sporting her cavewoman chic, Erica wheeled in a trolley full of champagne and buckets of ice.

'Have you ever had a bang?' Adam inquired of Chrissy mischievously. Grabbing two glasses and a bottle, he poured them both a drink. 'Here comes the interesting part,' he said and placed a plastic beer mat over his glass. 'You turn the glass upside down and bang it on the table. The champagne turns to froth and you drink it down in one. The bubbles go straight into your bloodstream. It's the best hit of alcohol you'll ever have.' And with that he slammed his own glass onto the table and swilled it down. 'Set 'em up, Joe.' Chrissy poured him a second glass and watched him repeat the exercise. After the third he let out an enormous, roaring belch.

Struggling to force down the dry, fizzy bubbles, Chrissy announced that one would be quite enough. But Adam was adamant. Half of the second glass went up her nose and she choked violently.

'Third time lucky, remember, all good things come in threes.'

She thought it was disasters that came in threes, but what the hell. She was beginning to get the hang of it.

A long, long time ago Mr Shinh, her physics teacher, had explained about infinity.

'Imagine that you are a blade of grass, growing in the middle of a football stadium. It might seem as though that stadium, and the sky above it, comprise the entire universe. But, as human beings, we know there is something beyond that stadium. Now imagine that our planet, our entire solar system, is a blade of grass and the universe, as we know it, is a football stadium.'

The fourteen-year-old Chrissy just hadn't been able to get her mind around that concept. Surely everything had to come to an end?

Not so. Arriving at the party, she had felt good. And after a line of coke she felt even better than that. And after a smoke and a few more lines of charlie she felt even better than that. And after the champagne bangs she felt so utterly wonderful there was only one thing left to do. Have another line of coke.

'Perhaps one day,' Mr Shinh had hypothesised, in one of his more abstract moods, 'thousands of years from now, human beings will evolve beyond their physical form.'

It was a theory that had greatly appealed to him. Probably because his own physical form served as something of a handicap. He was a 'Paki', British slang for 'lowest of the low'. But his was the only authority she had ever really looked up to and his philosophies were still very relevant to her. Especially at the moment. For, though she was using her mouth to speak and her hands to illustrate, the level of communication being reached was almost telepathic.

'I long to have a child.' She waved an arm majestically and the funny little Mediterranean man stared in silent wonder. 'I haven't used any birth control since 1975 and do you know what?' The funny little Mediterranean man shook his head. 'I can't seem to get pregnant.' She giggled. 'No, no let's be honest. In the last two years, I've had sex twice. Isn't that terrible? Once a year, Chrissy's libido comes out to play. Hello Mr Libido, and how are you today? In fact –' she hiccoughed and belched. 'Ooh, ha haa. Have you ever been banged, Mr Funny-Little-Mediterranean-Man? It is quite, quite delightful.

Perhaps I could inishinate – ininshiate – perhaps I could show you how it's done?'

'Excuse me, madam,' the funny little Mediterranean man's accent buzzed nasally. 'Do you have any idea who own the light blue Citroën parked outside?'

'You have to take me home,' Chrissy croaked, shaking Otto hard by the lapels of a jacket he hadn't been wearing when they arrived.

His head lolled lifelessly to one side and an elastic strand of saliva dangled from his mouth like a spider's thread.

'Come *on*.' She heaved him into a sitting position and his eyelids fluttered open. 'Can you take me home? Are you sober?' What a question to be asking at a quarter past ten in the morning.

As far as Chrissy could remember, the party had ground to a halt at around six. Otto was one of several other people who decided to crash in Adam's room.

'Hhnnnff.'

Chrissy hoped to God that she didn't look as bad as he did. She had an hour and three quarters in which to get home, clean up and get to work. It wasn't enough.

'I'll just go to the bog and then we'll leave,' Otto declared, surprisingly lucid.

Chrissy's coat was being used as a blanket by the same small, hairy person of indeterminate sex that he had been talking to earlier. Whisking the coat off the dormant womble, she slipped it on and waited for Otto. Considering the amount of booze she'd consumed, she couldn't understand why she didn't have a whopping great hangover. Whatever the reason, she was thankful for it.

Erica rolled into the space previously occupied by Otto and her left breast flopped inconveniently out of her suede boob tube and onto the rug.

Tiptoeing along the hall, Chrissy stopped outside the bathroom door and listened. Nothing. 'Otto? Are you all right? *Otto?*' She tried the handle. Locked. '*Otto.*' Banging and rattling the door, she began to get very worried. He hadn't looked at all well.

She lunged at the bathroom door in a vain attempt to break it down.

'A friend of mine at school taught me how to do this. He's in Wandsworth now, being detained at Her Majesty's pleasure.' Adam grinned energetically. No one had a right to look that good after only four hours sleep. 'Mind you, I can't see Lizzy getting much of a kick out of it, can you?'

'Er, no,' responded Chrissy, not having a clue as to what he was on about.

'We have to sit back to back and link arms. You put your feet against the door and I'll put mine against the wall.'

Chrissy did as she was told.

'Okay, on three, push as hard as you can. One. Two.' The wood around the lock creaked and splintered. 'Three!' The door flew open, smashed into the bathroom cabinet and swung back again. 'Good job he wasn't lying any closer to the door,' Adam chuckled. 'Instant decapitation.' He rose to his feet and walked over to where Otto lay unconscious.

'Is he all right?' Chrissy struggled to get up.

'No sweat,' Adam wheezed, heaving him over one shoulder in a fireman's lift.

After depositing Otto back in his room, he agreed to take her home. 'But first you must join me for some breakfast.'

'Adam, I'd love to but I simply haven't the time.'

'Nonsense,' he snapped, 'it won't take a minute.' He led her into the living room. 'Voilà.'

The place was spotless. Her eyes immediately searched for the cigarette butt she had irresponsibly ground into the carpet with her heel when no ashtrays had been readily available. All that remained was a vague orange stain. The LPs were back in their sleeves and stacked neatly beside the music centre. A woman's voice trilled operatically, accompanied by what sounded like a lute.

'Radio Three, man. Unbeatable.'

As far as Chrissy was concerned, classical music went in one ear and out the other but, she had to admit, it did make nice background music.

'Et voilà.' Flinging open the kitchen door, Adam bowed like a maître d'.

A mirror covered with several white lines lay on the kitchen table. Next to it, a bottle of champagne and a cup full of joints kept each other company.

'Le petit déjeuner est . . . ahh . . . fuck it. Never mind.' He grinned and his chin looked as though it was about to take off.

'Adam, you're incorrigible.'

'That's odd,' he said, 'I thought I was in Knightsbridge.'

The coke exploded and fizzed in the back of Chrissy's nose like sherbet. She dabbed her finger into the remnants of the line and rubbed it around her gums, which were already starting to go numb. Time stretched out before her in a series of long, white marble steps. She had absolute power over those steps and no matter how long she dallied on them, they would not make her late. Things were gradually coming together. For the next few hours she would be word perfect. If her mind thought of something stupid to say, her mouth would censor it. Every part of her body was bristling, alive and eager to co-operate.

Chrissy decided that her fears of riding pillion on Adam's motorbike had been completely unfounded. For a start she hadn't been aware that it was such a beautiful machine. On seeing the gleaming Kawasaki 750cc, snarling like a chromium dragon, her first instinct was to call the station, report sick and take off somewhere. Anywhere. And now, with her eyes streaming tears into the wind and juggernauts whipping within inches of her unprotected legs, Chrissy realised that there was more to life than drawing a pension at the end of it. Actually Adam was a very good driver barring one minor flaw. He seemed unable to cruise at less than seventy miles an hour.

'I'll 'ave you, you bastard. You're nicked, mate. I've got your fuckin' number,' the cabby, livid with rage, was screaming himself hoarse.

'They just can't handle it,' Adam shouted downwind, 'when somebody else starts taking the same liberties as they do.'

The cab, which had been dwindling in the distance as they

moved further and further away from it, stopped getting smaller. In fact, if anything, it was getting bigger. Turning the corner they skidded to a halt in front of the traffic lights bordering the top of the Fulham Road. Chrissy looked behind again. The cabby already had one foot out of his door. Slamming the door shut, he began running towards them. As he got to within grabbing distance, the lights changed and they roared into the Fulham Road. And stopped. Chrissy turned to see the cabby stomping back to his taxi, jabbing rabbit punches into the air as he went. Adam clicked the gears with his boot and they glided backwards to their original position in front of the traffic lights. Several drivers behind the cabby hooted their horns.

'Fuck off out of it,' he snarled. Just as he was getting in, he caught sight of them again. For a brief moment his irises rolled up into his head, leaving his eyes a pure, catatonic white. A new batch of traffic joined the tailback and the ensuing commotion was like an avant-garde rhapsody. Looking as though he was about to eat the steering wheel, the cabby drove the taxi to within inches of the back of the bike.

'Hey, bollock brain,' Adam shouted and clicked into first. 'Who rattled your cage?'

The cabby sprang out of the taxi like a bloated leopard. As they pulled into the Fulham Road for the second time, Adam insisted that they drive around the block, assuring Chrissy that there would be a real treat in store. Sure enough, the line of traffic hadn't moved. Mainly because the cabby was busy dragging the driver of the car behind him out onto the pavement and beating him up.

Having no time for a bath, Chrissy took off her blouse, washed her face, brushed her teeth, applied some roll-on deodorant to her armpits and put the blouse back on again. Trotting into Parson's Green tube station, she flashed her travel pass at the ticket collector, ran down the stone steps and straight into a waiting train. Unfortunately it was bound for High Street Kensington, so she had to get off and change at Earl's Court: 'District Line trains to Victoria and Charing Cross are running slightly behind schedule due to an incident on the line at Hammersmith.' In other words, some poor wretch had thrown themselves onto the track.

'Easily the best dance record made in the last twelve months, that was Heatwave and "Boogie Nights". This is Christine McArthur on LWS. Back in less than ninety seconds, after the news headlines.'

Whew, that was tough. Halfway through the show, Chrissy had been flying but now all she had was jet lag. She closed her eyes and drifted.

'– at midday tomorrow. Until then it's over to you.' Chrissy. Until then it's over to you, *Chrissy*.

'. . . ahh thank you, Jim. Now then it's – it's –' Chrissy shook herself awake and glanced frantically at the 45. Dammit. It was a white label. But whose? ' –a marvellous new single, guaranteed to curl your toes. At two minutes past the hour, this is Christine McArthur on LWS. But you can call me Chrissy.' She switched to intercom. 'What the hell's the matter with you?' she barked and Jim almost jumped out of his chair. 'I'm sorry,' she lowered her voice considerably.

'So am I,' Jim smiled and put his hand to the glass in an unselfconscious display of affection. 'It's just that when you didn't introduce me I thought –'

'Did I forget?'

'Yes.'

'Honestly, Jim, I didn't mean to.'

'Of course you didn't.'

Good, that was settled. 'Is your mother enjoying her stay?'

Jim let out a lengthy sigh. 'Have you ever had your mother to stay?'

'Oh God, yes. I can't think of anything worse.'

'Evidently I should have asked your advice before agreeing to it. You see, this is the first time and – well . . .'

'Hopefully the last?'

'Yes,' he breathed another sigh of relief, as though he hadn't expected her to understand. 'You've no idea what my father's death has done to her – well – perhaps you have –'

167

'You're darn tootin'.'

'– but she's become another person. Completely. We were never really that close but now – oh look Chrissy, I'm sorry.'

The needle was only halfway across the record. 'No, it's okay Jim, I'd like to hear what you have to say. It's like listening to myself when I was a kid.'

'Oh?'

That hadn't come out quite the way she intended. 'How much longer will she be staying?'

'Too long. A week, maybe more.'

Ouch. 'Would you like a chaperone one night this week?'

'You mean you?'

'I don't know what I can do exc–'

'Would you? That would be so fantastic.'

'Well it's nice to know that I'm wanted.'

Jim leaned into his microphone. 'I've often thought about you, Chrissy. I never asked you out because I didn't think you'd come. But just knowing you're willing to – listen . . . let's wait until my mother's gone. You can do without the aggravation, believe me.'

But that was the whole point. She wanted the aggro. At least, she wanted the chance to observe it objectively for a change. Suddenly this was turning into Peyton Place. 'I want to do it, really I do. It'll be interest–'

'No, I insist,' Jim said firmly. 'We'll go to a movie, you choose, and then we'll have dinner. Vegetarian,' he laughed.

'But I –'

'No.'

'Jim you –'

'Don't you want to?'

Dean Brando was positively exploding with zits today. He grinned weakly, acutely aware that his ace had been trumped by the cruel hand of fate. 'Coffee. *Medium* strong,' said Chrissy. He grinned again in a dumb sort of way that didn't suit him at all. Dunking a Mars Bar into her coffee, she gazed around the canteen. The carpet and walls were a dull, muted brown. The tables and chairs were arranged in such a way that the room was neither sparse nor cosy. Stifling central heating made it impossible to think clearly. No wonder she'd managed to get so depressed sitting here. Vegetating.

It was really a great movie. They both were. The scene in which Warren Beatty admitted that, 'Let's face it, I've fucked 'em all. It's what I do,' was worth the two pounds thirty-five admission price alone. But twenty minutes into *Bonnie and Clyde* Chrissy had begun to look at her watch.

'– in the Earl's Court Wimpy this lunchtime.'

'Yeah?'

'Two pros started arguing and one of them punched the other one right out of her chair.'

'You're kidding?'

'No, they rolled around on the floor for a while, scratching and pulling each other's hair. Meanwhile Tony, the cashier, just sits there like nothing is happening. Suddenly, there's a scream and the blonde one's face is covered with blood. She starts crying out, "I can't see, I can't bloody see."'

'And then what?'

'And then I done a runner. Everyone else was watching the fight so I had myself a free meal.' Jaz offered a plastic smile, like a TV game show host awaiting his 'spontaneous' applause.

'Oh look, there's Lila,' Otto announced, pretending he'd only just seen her. 'Excuse us, Jaz. We have some business to attend.'

'To,' Chrissy added quietly as they walked over to the other side of the bar.

'She's been telling that same story for months now. I think she must have a couple of rooms to let,' Otto said and tapped his temple, 'upstairs, you know?'

At ten-thirty the humidity in the Roebuck was unbearable. Freezing cold air gushed through the open windows to no avail. Chrissy sat next to the window watching Otto shoot yet another game of pool. Earlier on he had offered to teach her and she had accepted. Unfortunately he possessed none of Mr Shinh's talent for imparting knowledge. Instead, he proceeded to demonstrate the game by potting her balls as well as his own. And tutting whenever she missed an 'easy' shot. And purposely missing his own shots in a patronising attempt to make it 'fair'. He was quite good but no Hurricane Higgins.

'I think I'm going to leave,' she shouted over the jukebox.

'Now? Wait a minute.' After a brief discussion with his opponent, Otto handed his cue to a man in a light blue anorak, walked over to Chrissy and sat down. 'What's wrong?'

'Nothing. I just want to leave.'

'Where do you want to go?'

'Home.'

Otto chewed his lower lip thoughtfully. 'Me and Erica, we're not . . .'

Chrissy laughed good-naturedly. 'That's okay, you don't have to explain to me.'

'Do you want me to come along? I'll drive you.'

'No. I could do with the walk. There's not much fresh air up here.'

She descended the short flight of steps and walked into the downstairs bar just as Erica came in from the street. Nodding towards the bar, Chrissy fished out her purse. 'Drink?'

'Thanks. Bushmills.'

Chrissy raised her eyebrows. 'Make that two,' she said. The pale orange firewater hit the back of her throat and she caught her breath, 'Do you drink this stuff all the time?'

Erica smiled. She was dressed slightly more seasonally, but no less unconventionally, in a tartan three-piece suit and tie. None of the tartans matched. 'Only when I can afford it. Otherwise it's strictly Special Brew. Still, I shouldn't think you have many money problems.'

'No more so than anyone else,' said Chrissy, remembering her short stint as a solicitor's secretary. 'What do you do?'

'Not a lot, I'm afraid,' Erica laughed. 'I design my own jewellery –'

'Really?' Chrissy cooed with genuine interest.

'– but I'm having a lot of trouble finding an outlet. I really ought to set up a stall in Kenny market or something but, I don't know, it's the organisation, isn't it? I'm not very good at that sort of thing.'

'Have you ever come across Julia Hazlebury?'

'Ah well,' Erica shrugged, 'you see, that's just the kind of contact I need to –'

'She's a friend of mine. What sort of things do you make?'

Putting her hand to the side of her head, Erica waggled an earlobe.

'They're gorgeous,' Chrissy marvelled. A blue onyx sat like an eagle's eye in the centre of a silver shield. African style tribal markings were carved around the rim of the shield in an intricate, asymmetrical pattern.

'Here,' said Erica, slipping the earrings off.

'Oh no, I couldn't.'

'On one proviso. That you wear them the next time you see Ms Hazlebury.'

'I will, I will.' Chrissy accepted the earrings and put them on, squinting left and right to try and see what they looked like on her.

'They really suit you.' She meant it, too. 'You haven't seen Adam by any chance? He seems to have disappeared.'

'Not since this morning. Otto's upstairs.'

For several moments they sat in silence. The bell for last orders clanged officiously.

A bunch of squaddies whistled and shouted as Chrissy walked past them. Poor sods. There were no real wars left to fight. The best they could look forward to was a stint in Northern Ireland, Britain's Vietnam. Except that these empty-headed bulldogs had willingly volunteered. One too many Clint Eastwood movies, perhaps. A panda cruised parallel with her for a few seconds and then moved on. What with the constant police presence and bright, twenty-four hour window displays, the King's Road was one of the safest places in London. The squaddies staggered off down the road in search of a curry that they could consume and then regurgitate.

As Chrissy boarded the train, a man slipped in beside her. They moved to opposite ends of the otherwise empty carriage and she sat down. In the corner of her eye she noticed that the man had remained standing. The skin around his eyes was deeply discoloured as though he'd been looking through a pair of joke binoculars.

'Mine oh,' a dislocated voice crackled over the Tannoy as the doors slammed shut and the train lurched into the tunnel.

Abruptly, the lights blacked out. Seconds later they came on again. The man had moved closer, she was sure of it. The lights blacked out again and the train squealed slowly to a halt in the tunnel.

Straining to make out any movement amongst the static shapes of the seats, Chrissy could see nothing. She held her breath and listened as the train hummed gently. Gradually the hum faded into silence. There was a faint click. Suddenly the man was towering over her and in his left hand he held a long metal blade.

'Show me,' he grinned.

Chrissy looked him straight in the eye and began unbuttoning her blouse. 'You won't be needing the knife.'

Seventeen

I'm late, I'm late, for a very important date. Jack churned the words over in his mind, trying desperately to remember where he was and what was going on. The room. It was Lydia's. The bed. Ditto. Ah hah, one mystery solved. Question number two, where was she?

'Are you awake?'

'Yes.' Where was that voice coming from?

'Come down here and help me. I've lost a lens.'

Leaning over the edge of the bed, Jack scrutinised the scenery.

'Never mind about my goddamn ass, get down here.'

'Morning, Lydia.' Jack stuck his head under the bed. Now she looked like a blind, drowned rat.

'Be careful, you might step on it or something. It's a tiny, transparent lens. Can you see it?'

Running his hand lightly over the rug. Jack felt for the lens. 'No. Listen Lydia, there's something I've been meaning to ask you. It's –'

'Don't worry, I'm clean. Now can you see it or not? I've got to be out of here by noon.'

'Noon! What time is it?'

'Eleven fifteen.'

'My plane leaves at noon! If I don't – I can't . . . Lydia, it's been wonderful, what can I say. Please, I'll write to you. I have everything – yes . . .'

Lydia stood, skinny and sleepy, in a large white vest. 'You'll never make it.'

'Oh God, I'll never make it.'

'I don't fucking believe it,' Jack muttered murderously. The plastic upholstery squeaked and scraped beneath his clawing fingers. He prayed for Señor Loco, his niece Rosa, any goddamn one who had a driving licence and was prepared to go faster than forty. This lame brained old fart – what was his name? Matthew Kropotkin? What the hell kind of a name was that anyway? What was he trying to do, get into the Guinness Book of Records?

'Ahm,' Jack cleared his throat. 'Could you possibly go a little faster. My plane leaves at noon.'

'S-sure. S-s-sure,' the old fart stuttered and revved all the way up to forty-three miles an hour.

Even including the case of the vanishing wallet, this trip could be counted as a success but not if he blew another ton by missing the fucking plane. Incredibly, signs for the airport began to appear. Five miles to go. 'Do you have the time, please?'

'S-sure. S-s-sure,' the old fart drawled and then fell silent.

'Well? What is it? *What's the time*?' he bellowed, finally realising his driver's real handicap.

'S-sure. S-s-sure.'

Taking a deep swig of duty free Jack Daniels, Jack breathed a sigh of relief. The plane had been late taking off. The adjacent seat was empty so he folded away the connecting arm and put his legs up. Today's movie had Woody Allen in it. Great.

Eighteen

Colin sat with the old man eating breakfast.

'Oi, I want a word wiv you,' Colin declared loudly, as Andy came in.

'Shut yer bleedin' row.' Spittle flew from the old man's lips and tongue.

'Wassall this about you and some spade slag, eh?' Colin persisted.

'Will you belt up and –' The old man leapt out of his chair and spun to face Andy. 'You dirty little toerag, what 'ave you been up to?' He fingered his belt buckle, breathing heavily, and grinned to show the decayed brown and green stubs.

In a flash Colin was standing between then and waving a blue piece of paper in front of the old man's nose. 'Keep your 'ands off 'im and go and get drunk. You know it makes sense,' his voice rose and fell in pitch as though he were singing.

'I'll see you later,' the old man warned, wagging his finger at Andy.

'Not if I see you first,' Andy mumbled under his breath. ''Oo saw me?' he asked as the front door slammed shut.

'Never you mind. So it's true then is it?' A sly smirk spread across Colin's face. It was rare that the old man got mad at Andy.

'I just wanna know where, that's all.'

'Outside some pub in Chelsea, that's where. Snoggin'.' Colin feigned a look of pure disgust. 'Must be like puttin' your tongue up someone's arse.'

You stupid cunt, thought Andy, what would you know about it? 'Must've been somebody else, I 'aven't been up that way in weeks.' He was betting on the fact that Colin hadn't seen it himself.

'Oh yeah?' Colin's grand moment of triumph was slipping away from him. 'Oh yeah?' he said, more loudly this time. 'Well where you bin goin' then?' His eyes went misty and his head began to twitch.

Andy loped along the fourth floor balcony of Clem Attlee House in search of number forty-three. Some coloured geezer had jumped from here a few weeks ago and broken both his legs. The old man reckoned the bloke knew it wasn't high enough to kill himself and did it for the insurance. 'Typical spade trick.'

Peering over the low wall to the concrete courtyard below, Andy found it hard to believe that anyone could be so desperate. When they were kids he and his brother used to hang from this wall, daring each other to let go with one hand, but even Colin wasn't that thick.

Mrs O'Day answered the door. 'If it's Carl you're looking for, I'm afraid he's not here.' Her soft Irish brogue and ample bosom caused Andy to wonder whether it was usual to want to knob your best mate's old dear. 'Would you be wanting to wait?' She held the door open, half-expectantly.

'Any idea where 'e's got to?'

'If you boys had any brains, you'd still be at school and then you wouldn't have to be looking for each other,' she laughed good-naturedly and went on, 'I can't be standing here all day, are you coming in or no?' Her eyes were saying something that her mouth was not but Andy was in a hurry. 'Try the caff,' she shouted after him. Where else?

Amongst the greasy cabbies and balding pensioners, four neatly cropped heads stood out like an oasis in a desert. Madge had seen him coming and was already making her way around the counter.

'Before you say anyfink, I'm not stoppin' so keep yer 'air on.'

She had never forgiven him for the incident involving a bottle of brown sauce.

'That's a fine one coming from you, that is. And take your bloody merry men with you an' all. They've been in here since ten o'clock with –'

'Two cups a' tea between 'em,' Andy chorused. 'Yeah, yeah I know.' A sausage sandwich wouldn't have gone amiss but he knew better than to antagonise the only cafe proprietor in the area that didn't have a complete ban on skinheads. Carl and the others trooped out slowly; as he passed the fretting Madge, Spig goosed her. She let fly a torrent of expletives before officially barring any customer who had less than a quarter of an inch of hair on his head.

'Oh well done, Spiggot, whaddya do for an encore? You *pill*ock,' Carl rasped venomously.

'Wassit matter ay? 'Oo gives a monkey's about that old cow?'

'Spig?'

'What?'

'S'pose I was to knock your teef so far down the back a' your froat, you ended up 'avin' to talk fru' yer arse.' He turned to Andy. 'First it's you and yer fuckin' shit sandwiches, now this. Why do I bovver? Anyway, where you bin? We bin waitin' for ya.'

'Yeah, where you bin?' Spig piped up, 'we bin waitin' ages.'

'Why?' He didn't really need to ask. The atmosphere crackled like static electricity on a nylon sweater, it looked as though 1978 was gonna kick off with a bang.

'We *were* plannin' on gettin' some grub down our necks,' Carl said calmly and deliberately did not look at Spig, 'before rumblin' the Roebuck.'

'Where'sat?' Andy replied instinctively. A black cab buzzed along the road towards the five skins as they straggled on the pavement outside the caff. A part of Andy ran to the kerb, hailed the taxi and drove off, never to return.

'Oh do come in, Andy, the *Roe*buck. We bin up there more 'n once.'

Andy smacked his palm against his forehead. 'Course I 'member. We seen them 'Ell's Angels layin' into each uvver, didn't we? Gordon Bennett, yuge bastards they were. You 'member one of 'em was tryin' a' rip that bird's jeans off. Fuckin' funny, that was.'

'Angels?' Spig's voice wavered. 'Listen, my old man – it's the Road 'Ogs yer on about innit?'

'Yeah,' Andy affirmed.

'Yeah well my old man's had real bovver from them. 'E reckons they're all but the fuckin' Mafia when it comes to –'

''Old on, 'old on,' Carl droned over the mutterings of increasing trepidation, 'there's no need to wet yourselves, there ain't gonna be no Road 'Ogs.'

'You should've 'eard what 'e 'ad to say about –' Spig started.

'*Because*,' without raising the volume of his voice one decibel, Carl uttered the word powerfully enough to shatter a diamond, 'they never go there at lunchtime, only in the ev'nin'. And we, that is those of us with any bottle, will be arrivin' at approximately one p.m. Now then Spig, how would you describe one p.m.? I mean what part of the day is it? Mornin'? Ev'nin'?'

'Afternoon,' mumbled Spig.

'Thank you, Spig.'

The World's End was anything but, with a teeming community and a friendly atmosphere except, of course, for the blacks who lived on the local council estate. It was a quarter to one and they were less than five minutes walk away from the Roebuck.

'We're gonna give them punks a good lickin',' said Carl, savouring every word. 'Hit the upstairs bar, that's where they all 'ang out.'

Including Grace. How was Andy going to stop her from being mashed? The thought of it made him ill. Murmurs of approval rippled through the rest of the crew. Andy took a mental head count. Sixteen. As well as the amassed Churchill skins there were nine others who'd joined up en route. Everywhere you looked these days, there were skins. A feeling of pride welled up inside him. Grace would be somewhere else today, he was sure of it. Absolutely, positively, damn well sure of it.

'Listen Andy, I've got to go. I wish you could hear me, Andy. Andy?'

That smell. It was like clean laundry mixed with chalk. Wherever he was, it certainly wasn't home. The sheets on the bed were coarse, crisp and crinkly, they were also tucked in much too tightly and Andy strained against them in an effort to turn over and go back to sleep.

'Andy, are you awake? Can you hear me?'

A searing bolt of pain shot down the left side of his face as he tried to open his eyes. Gingerly, he tried opening just the right eye and, with some difficulty, succeeded. Next to his bed there was a large window and through it he could see trees silhouetted against the night sky. He watched the hardy perennials bend back and forth in the breeze and gradually he drifted into half sleep. Something blocked his view of the trees.

'Andy, it's me, Grace. They're going to throw us out soon, can you hear me?'

'Groan?' he asked, but the left side of his mouth refused to play ball.

'Oh, Andy, what have they done to you?'

Who? What had who done to him? Flapping and waving with his right hand, he indicated that he wanted to be helped up.

'Lean forward,' said Grace and an arrow dug into his heart as he did so. Reclining on the rearranged pillows, Andy smiled, deliberately dragging up the left corner of his mouth. 'Oh, Andy, what were you doing? I got your telephone call and so I went to the downstairs bar. I couldn't believe it when you all came charging in like that, the upstairs bar is a total wreck. I don't understand why you did it. Why?'

A few blocks away from the Roebuck, Andy let himself slip to the back of the striding pack of skins, dodged round the corner and into a phone box. Fucking lucky this was Chelsea and not Fulham otherwise the directories would have been ripped out yonks ago. Feverishly, he ran his finger down the Rs. Rodrigues, Rodriguez – fuckin' Ities, come on – Rodwell, Roe – here we go – Christ, they can't be more than a couple of blocks away now – Roebuck, The, 15 Pond Street – no, fuck it, that wasn't it – King's Road, here we go. Three five two . . . racing along the pavement, Andy caught up with the tail end of the crew just as the first few went bundling through the door. The patrons stared open-mouthed as they stampeded through the downstairs bar and up the stairs. Where was Grace, he couldn't see her? The front detail rushed into the upstairs bar while the rear gunners proceeded to demolish the toilets on the landing. Andy watched as six Dr Marten boots kicked the toilet doors off their hinges and there was a scream as an occupant met with a face full of painted wood. Didn't sound like Grace so he hurtled through the door to join his mates and – uhh. Why was it that when you're about to be the victim of violence, everything goes into slow motion? Standing to the left of the doorway a colossal bear of a man wielded a sawn-off pool cue, just waiting for the next skin to come through. He wore a baseball cap turned the wrong way round and blood poured from his nose. Glass exploded everywhere as windows were smashed and the pinball machine was up-ended and thrown to the floor. 'Yew filthy scumbag son of a bitch,' the barman bellowed and began to swing. Low. A punk girl tottered helplessly about in the middle of the mayhem screaming at the top of her voice. 'Stop it! Stop it! Pleease.' She was rewarded with a kick in the mouth from Carl, who stood on top of a pool table brandishing a sock full of pool balls, and she fell to the floor, dribbling blood down her fishnet top. Whumpf. Winded, Andy doubled over. The barman pulled the cue back and prepared to swing again. Several punks pushed past Andy, hurrying to get away. But Carl, foreseeing this stratagem, had made sure that there was no escape. The rear gunners would 'ave 'em. Glass sprayed from the back of the barman's head as the cavalry came to Andy's rescue but the pool cue kept on coming. Yards, then feet, then inches away from his bowed head. A last look at the punkette lying on the floor in a pool of blood, spitting teeth and heaving spasmodically.

The hospital ward had six beds, two rows of three, facing each other. Apart from Andy there were four old men, each with his own set of visitors, and a boy about his age, who looked as though he'd just come out of the army. At regular half-minute intervals, the old man furthest away from Andy erupted like a human volcano, spraying, and spewing from every orifice imaginable and the noise that accompanied this display made Cap Spas' '*geeeeuggggh*' sound like someone politely clearing their throat.

'Whanf?' Andy asked, pointing to his head. His left side wasn't completely numb but he had to think about moving, it didn't come naturally.

'I don't know. They're keeping you in for observation.'

Fuck it, that meant the pigs'd be sniffing round soon. 'Tsssime?' Andy managed and held up his right hand. Instead of his digital watch, around his wrist was a plastic strap with his surname on it.

'It's nearly eight thirty, I'll have to go any second. What were you doing up there? I saw Nick, I told him you weren't with the rest of them, that you were with me. He helped you into the back room until the police had been and gone, do you remember?'

'Nnnfh.'

'No, you were really out of it. You should've seen the place afterwards, they took Jaz away on a stretcher.'

'Harr?' Andy waved his hand and moved his eyes from side to side. It hurt.

'Nick brought you here in his car, he's been ever so good. He asked me to say sorry but, you know, the way you look and everything – anyway, what *were* you doing? Was it a gang war or something? Nick said they were letting some people go and concentrating on the punks.'

'Nnnfh,' Andy dipped his head to the right in an attempt to nod.

'Why? What had they done?'

Nothing. Absolutely nothing. To his knowledge, the attack on the pub was simply a show of strength. A rumble. A laugh.

The Human Volcano's visitors got up to leave and the rest of the visitors quickly followed suit. Shuffling off sombrely, they all shot their respective hosts a parting glance, as if they expected sudden death to occur imminently. And, judging from the patients, they weren't far wrong.

'It's a shame that boy didn't have any visitors,' Grace whispered. 'He must feel really left out.'

'I lerb ye,' said Andy.

Grace's eyes filled with tears and she squeezed his hand.

He could hardly feel it. 'Wharva nn sisshu?'

'Angie? Oh she's all right, don't worry about her. I left her at the flat with Otto, she's safe enough. Though God knows what's going to happen when Jack gets back. He's due any moment. I'll probably have to keep her under lock and key. It's a good job she wasn't there when it happened. Oh, Andy,' the corners of her mouth twitched and tugged downwards, 'what a way to start the New Year. You're all . . . you're all . . . broken up.' Though her breathing remained calm and regular, tears trickled around the side of her nose and collected in a puddle on top of her lip.

Something clunked against the ward doors and they swung open revealing a nurse pushing a trolley full of bedpans and coloured pills.

'And what, may I ask, are you doing here, young lady? Visiting hours are over.' Her clipped, cold Welsh accent was at odds with her sunny West Indian features and Andy wondered whether she was related to Shirley Bassey.

'I'm sorry, he's been out cold. He's only just this minute woken up.'

'Well all right then,' she snapped but her eyes were kind. 'You can stay while I give out this medication but no longer.'

'Thanks.'

'Nnnfh,' Andy agreed and tensed his left cheek in an agonising wink.

'Next up we have a single, released late last year, by a relatively unknown group. To be honest with you I didn't rate it at the time but . . . well judge for yourselves.' Reaching over to the small metal box on the wall beside his bed, the boy next to Andy dialled his headphones up full. 'You're listening to Capital Radio one-nine-four and here's a brief warning to anybody out there who is under the impression that they're indispensable.'

We don't need you, we don't need you, we don't need you, any of you . . .

MICHAEL CHABON

THE MYSTERIES OF PITTSBURGH

Art Bechstein steps out of the library into the summer of his graduation year, a season that lies between a past full of secrets and a future of hard-won experience.

Art's father wants his son to become a respectable adult, even though his own discreet 'business' is that of a gangster. But Art, not yet ready for respectability, falls in with the exotic, charming Arthur Lecomte, and ricochets between a homosexual relationship and an intense affair with a strange and beautiful girl called Phlox. Before long, the world of his new friends and the underworld of his father must collide, with consequences that Art cannot control.

THE MYSTERIES OF PITTSBURGH is a remarkable debut from one of the most talented new writers of recent years.

URSULA BENTLEY

PRIVATE ACCOUNTS

B. J. Berkely is a woman full of certainties.

Arriving from the States to spend a year in Switzerland with her physicist husband, she knows all about the smug, conformist, unliberated nature of Swiss society. She knows also that she represents all that is dynamic, free-thinking and uninhibited in American culture.

All this and more, B. J. Berkely knows. And when B. J. Berkely is sure of a thing, she acts. Switzerland – perhaps, in due course, the whole of Europe – is about to be catapulted into the twentieth century.

'Ursula Bentley's brilliant, bustling novel'
The Guardian

'Compulsive reading . . . Bentley uses her characters as a dramatist might: when it is not their turn to speak you are none the less aware that everyone has a part to play'
The Times Literary Supplement

'Ursula Bentley's hilarious PRIVATE ACCOUNTS is her long-awaited second novel; its deft, gentle caricature matches the exact timing of its Swiss setting'
New Statesman

'Ursula Bentley has a piercing eye for female frailty and in her new novel she turns it to hilarious account'
The Irish Times

RICHARD RUSSO

MOHAWK

MOHAWK chronicles over a dozen lives in a decaying leather town in upstate New York. It is a picture of life which is true for the whole world, and once viewed, will never be forgotten. It puts into words what many of us feel but few can say.

'This book is too skilful for a first novel'
John Irving

'An immensely readable and sympathetic novel. Mr Russo has an instinctive gift for capturing the rhythms of small-town life'
New York Times

'Russo's natural grace as a storyteller is matched by his compassion for his characters. MOHAWK is lively reading; it is a painful story, yet it is told with great mischief – and the triumphs and the tragedies of the characters are enhanced as victories and defeats always are, by wit'
John Irving

'MOHAWK is singular and brilliant'
Bill Buford of Granta

'Russo writes with sensitivity and insight and many of his characters are vivid and eccentric'
The Irish Times

'One of the most refreshing first novels to come along in years'
Boston Herald

Current and forthcoming titles from Sceptre

MICHAEL CHABON
THE MYSTERIES OF PITTSBURGH

URSULA BENTLEY
PRIVATE ACCOUNTS

RICHARD RUSSO
MOHAWK

J. M. O'NEILL
OPEN CUT
DUFFY IS DEAD

BOOKS OF DISTINCTION